D0007737

FOR YOUNG READERS

THE TRUE STORY OF A STOLEN DOG AND THE HUMANS HE BROUGHT TOGETHER

STEVEN J. CARINO
AND ALEX TRESNIOWSKI

An Imprint of Thomas Nelson

ISBN 978-1-4002-2357-2 (audiobook)
ISBN 978-1-4002-2356-5 (eBook)

Library of Congress Cataloging-in-Publication Data

Names: Carino, Steven J, author. | Tresniowski, Alex, author. | Teplow, Rotem, illustrator.
Title: Oliver for young readers : the true story of a stolen dog and the humans he brought together / Steven J. Carino and Alex Tresniowski ; illustration by Rotem Teplow.
Description: Nashville, TN : Thomas Nelson, 2021. | Audience: Ages 8-12 |
Summary: "An inspirational true story about a dog and the community who saved him, Oliver for Young Readers by Steven Carino and Alex Tresniowski reminds kids that their own acts of kindness have the power to change lives"-- Provided by publisher.
Identifiers: LCCN 2020036691 (print) | LCCN 2020036692 (ebook) | ISBN 9781400223541 (hardcover) | ISBN 9781400223565 (epub)
Subjects: LCSH: Lost dogs--United States--Anecdotes--Juvenile literature. | Dog owners--United States--Biography--Juvenile literature. | Human-animal relationships--Juvenile literature.
Classification: LCC SF427.6 .C375 2021 (print) | LCC SF427.6 (ebook) | DDC 636.70092/9--dc23
LC record available at https://lccn.loc.gov/2020036691
LC ebook record available at https://lccn.loc.gov/2020036692
ISBN 978-1-4002-2354-1

Written by Steven J. Carino and Alex Tresniowski
Illustration of Oliver by Rotem Teplow
Cover photograph by Shaina Fishman

Printed in the USA
21 22 23 24 25 PC/LSCC 6 5 4 3 2 1

Mfr: PC/LSCC / Crawfordsville, IN / December 2020 / PO #12040407

*To my mother, Marie Carino, for always
making me feel like your special boy*

*To my father, Nunzie Carino, for showing
me the value of hard work*

*To my brother, Frank Carino, for teaching
me all about the love of music*

Contents

Contents

Foreword

It was June 2, 1963, and I was waiting impatiently for my father's car to pull into the driveway of our home in Long Island. My sisters, Nancy and Annette, and my brother Frank were waiting with me. It was such an exciting day for us, and deep down we all hoped the new addition to our family might make things better.

Three days earlier we received word that our brother Steven had finally arrived. Our parents told us over and over that Steven was "a very big boy." I was twelve years old, and I took them literally. So as I waited to finally get a look at him, I expected him to be a giant baby.

All my parents meant was that Steven weighed nine pounds, eight ounces, and was twenty-one inches long. So when he finally came home, I could not believe how tiny he was. In an instant I fell madly in love with my baby brother. I felt a deep and immediate bond to him. I attached myself to my mother's hip and helped her take care of Steven in any way I could. I couldn't get enough of him. I have to admit that sometimes when Steven was sleeping, I'd sneak into my parents' bedroom and wake him up. Then I would scream, "Steven is crying. I'll get him!"

Over the years, our bond grew stronger. Even as our lives went in different directions, we maintained our special bond. And we still make a point to see each other once a week.

We share so many interests, and one of them is our mutual love of dogs. Steven's many dogs have always meant the world to him, as have mine. Neither of us has children, and we both think of our dogs as our babies. We think of them as our best friends—aside from each other, that is.

On February 12, 2019, two days before Valentine's Day, Steven and his dog, Oliver, came to my home for dinner. As usual, Steven and I sat in the kitchen and talked while Oliver sat in my dining room, barking. Steven called for Oliver to come, even though he knew he wouldn't—for some strange reason, Oliver was afraid of my dark kitchen floor. Steven tried to bribe him with treats, but it was no use. Oliver refused to budge. Oliver was afraid of a lot of things, and he particularly hated when either Steven or I raised our voices or there were loud sounds. He liked it when things were calm. I think it had to do with Oliver's peaceful life on a farm with his best buddy, Steven.

Two days later my home phone rang a little after 11:00 p.m. It was Steven. I knew he liked to stay up late, but he never called after ten. I immediately knew something was wrong, and Steven confirmed it: Oliver was missing.

Oliver, the sweet little dog who helped lift Steven out of the lowest point in his life, who was Steven's best friend and brightest light, who brought him joy and love and purpose and sometimes even the resolve to go on. The dog whose sudden disappearance, I feared, might break Steven's spirit and take away the funny, positive, caring brother I knew and cherished. That was the last thing I ever wanted to happen, and even then, on the day Oliver vanished, I knew we might need a miracle to prevent it. But then, how often do miracles actually happen?

What follows is Steven's story of the incredible events that happened after Oliver disappeared. I was with Steven for most of those events. (I have been with him for many of the highs and lows of his life, and he has always been there for me too.) In many ways I am still my mother's little helper, doing what I can to look after my baby bother. I wouldn't want it any other way.

As the story unfolds, you may recognize something I call *invisible threads*. I think these are the unbreakable bonds that connect human beings to each other, no matter who they are or where they come from. You may marvel at the power of community—of the incredible things that are possible when people come together in bad times. I hope you will see the love and gentleness of my brother, just as I do, and I hope you will learn something from his story, just as I did.

And, finally, I hope the story of Steven and Oliver leads you to be extra thankful for your own invisible thread connections that bind you to the people or pets that fill your heart with love.

LAURA SCHROFF, AUTHOR OF #1 *NEW YORK TIMES* BESTSELLER

AN INVISIBLE THREAD

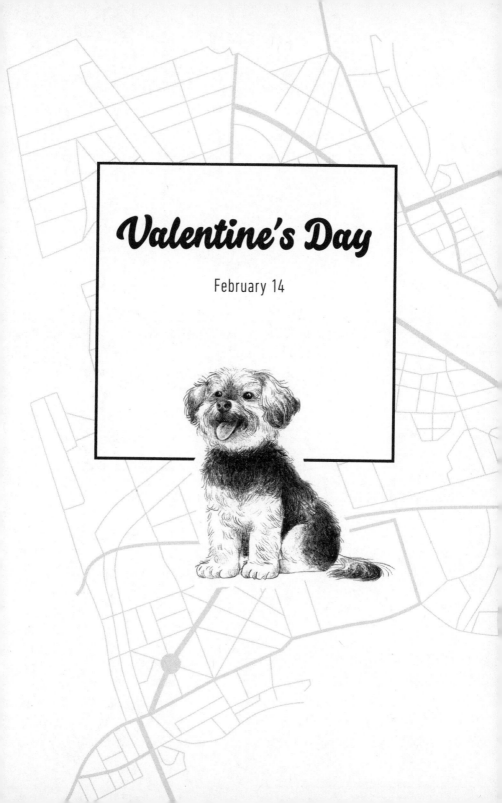

Valentine's Day

February 14

Chapter 1

You know that feeling when something bad happens and for a minute you think you might be dreaming? Like it didn't actually happen, or maybe it was someone's idea of a joke? Well, that's exactly the feeling I got when I realized my beloved pet dog, Oliver—my best friend in the whole world—was missing. I thought, *Obviously, this can't be happening. Obviously, Oliver must be here somewhere.*

But it *was* happening. And Oliver *was* missing.

Let me back up a bit from that terrible day and introduce myself. My name is Steven, and I'm a driver. I drive people from place to place in my small corner of the world in New York State. I drive them everywhere: to airports, hotels, office buildings, weddings, parties, colleges, hockey practices, you name it.Driving is my job, and I do it well—and I like doing it.

Maybe it started when I was ten or eleven years old, and my father used to let me sit up in the passenger seat of our beige Chrysler on family trips and help him with directions. This was long before Google Maps or GPS or anything like that. I'd unfold a big map and figure out what highway we needed to get on, and I'd tell my dad when to turn.

"Dad, the Cross County Parkway is coming up," I'd say. "You need to get on Central Avenue and take the first exit."

"Cross County Parkway? You sure about that, Steven?"

"Yes, I'm sure, Dad."

"Okay, then. Here we go."

He called me his "little navigator," and that made me feel like he was proud of me, which I really liked, because Dad didn't always make us kids feel good about ourselves. He could get into bad moods and say mean things—but that's a whole other story. When he let me be his navigator and I led him from highway to highway, Dad and I made a great team. So maybe that's why I like driving so much.

One thing I don't love about driving is traffic, and on the miserable day I lost Oliver, the traffic was really bad. It had snowed that week, and snow on the roads always slows things down in the New York City area, which is where I live and work. I had to drive one of my regular clients from Mount Kisco, a suburb of the city, to the JFK Airport in the borough of Queens, a forty-seven-mile trip. Normally, the drive would take about seventy-five minutes, but that day I budgeted two full hours. I made it to the airport in time, but just barely.

Then, on the way back to my home in Bedford, another New York City suburb, the traffic was so heavy that it took me almost an hour to move all of two miles. *Two miles!* I didn't get back to the one-room cottage where I lived until 3:00 p.m., which left me almost no time at all to get ready for my next job—a pick-up in the nearby town of Katonah and a drive into midtown Manhattan, a place known for its never-ending bumper-to-bumper traffic.

All of which is to say, I was left without any time at all to spend even a few minutes with my funny, adorable, twelve-pound Yorkie–Shih Tzu mix, Oliver. Which meant Oliver would be stuck inside all day by himself. Now, Oliver knows that sometimes he has to stay home by himself. Before I leave, I always turn on the TV for him because he loves watching dog food commercials and barking when the dogs appear on the screen. He even knows some commercials by heart and barks before the dogs appear! So Oliver is okay on his own—but still, I try never to leave him home by himself for a whole day if I can help it. Maybe it's because I miss him more than he misses me.

Oliver's Thoughts

When my dad leaves, he puts the TV on. That's how I know he is going to work. Then I can watch the doggie commercials and bark at them without getting yelled at!

Anyway, I thought about the hard drive ahead of me, and I thought about Oliver's long day alone, and I had an idea. I looked up the phone number of my next client, Mrs. Durant, and tapped out a text message to her on my cell:

> Do you mind if I bring my dog, Oliver, with me for our drive? It's Valentine's Day, and he hasn't seen me all day. I promise you won't even know he's there.

I'm not the kind of guy who worries about what people think of my dog and me. I wasn't embarrassed about not wanting to leave Oliver alone on Valentine's Day. I happily admit to anyone that Oliver is my best friend. I know that so-called "dog people" will understand my relationship with Oliver, but I also know that others might not. Some people might think a man who dotes on his dog and calls him his best friend and worries about leaving him alone on Valentine's Day is, well, maybe a bit eccentric, which means unusual.

I know that. I just don't care.

The fact is, Oliver and I are a great fit. It's really as simple as that. Me, the talkative guy with the New York accent who doesn't tell a story so much as acts it out with his whole body

Oliver and I are a great fit.

and who loves singing along to old Elvis Presley records, and Oliver, the rascally little fellow with big round eyes, so playful and loving and *good with people* and yet so scared of the tiniest noise.

Steven and Oliver. Oliver and Steven. Always together, take 'em or leave 'em.

Oliver's Thoughts

I love when my dad puts on his records as he makes us food in the morning. I hop on the bed and pretend I can understand the lyrics. Then he comes over and gives me a hug.

It's been that way with dogs and me since I was ten years old and my mother got really sick—and I turned to our medium-sized Yorkie Terrier, Michael, for support.

My mom was a sweet and wonderful woman who dearly loved her five children—my three older sisters, Annette, Laura, and Nancy; my older brother, Frankie; and me, Steven. I was the youngest child, and I was five years younger than any of the other kids. Because of that age difference, and as my brother and sisters got older and started making friends of their own, my mother was able to spend a lot of time with me. For much of my childhood, my mother was not only my teacher, cheerleader, play partner, and protector; she was also my best friend. I knew as long as my mother was around, I would be okay.

But when she got sick, I grew closer to Michael and then to one of his puppies, a little Shorkie named Marcie. After my mom passed away, Marcie would sleep only with me, and I felt very comforted by her presence and loyalty and devotion. This was the first time I recognized the power of a dog's love.

Since then, I've always had a very special relationship with my dogs. They have never been just pets to me.

They were my friends—sometimes my only friends.

I heard a ping on my cell phone. Mrs. Durant had answered my text message.

Yes, of course. Bring Oliver along!

I'd never taken Oliver on a job with me before. It wasn't the professional thing to do. But since Mrs. Durant didn't seem to mind, I was suddenly very excited to have him with me for the long drive. It felt like an unexpected Valentine's Day present for us both.

When I finally got back to my cottage in Bedford, I opened the front door and called out to Oliver.

"Come on, boy. We're going to the city!"

Oliver jumped off the bed and barked and spun around in circles and made it look like he understood we were going somewhere special, when in fact I know he would have been just as utterly overjoyed to take a walk with me to the end of the street and back.

An Oliver Story

I believe that Oliver thinks my name is Stee. Not Steve or Steven, just Stee. When he hears the first part of my name, he starts bouncing and barking, and the rest of my first name doesn't even matter! So to Oliver, I'm just Stee!

Chapter 2

The drive into Manhattan with Mrs. Durant was as bad as I had feared. The Henry Hudson Parkway wasn't that crowded, but once I entered the city, it was bumper-to-bumper traffic. Driving in Manhattan had always been an endurance test, but lately it seemed it was worse than ever. But since there was nothing I could do about it, why get twisted out of shape? I had Sam Cooke playing softly on the radio, and I was enjoying my conversation about music with Mrs. Durant.

And I had Oliver on my lap.

Oliver's Thoughts

I'm not sure where we are, but these buildings are so big! We are driving so slowly. It's so much fun looking out the window. I'm really glad Stee took me with him today.

I finally got to Mrs. Durant's hotel on Sixth Avenue in mid-town. Then, in the darkness of early evening, I got back in my car for the long, slow drive back to Bedford.

When I was four years old, my mother helped me learn the names of all the US presidents. That is my first memory of being alive, or maybe my second, after the time I sat with my little red Show 'N Tell record player and stared in wonder at the record spinning around and producing this amazing sound. I can't be sure I remember the song that was playing—maybe "Barbara Ann" by the Beach Boys?—but I definitely still remember the presidents.

We'd sit on the wooden steps that led up to the kitchen in our house, and my mother would break out the big encyclopedia—the volume with *P*, for presidents. It was 1967, and back then there were only thirty-six presidents. My mother and I would flip through all these pictures of old men in ruffled white shirts with wild gray hair. One by one I learned their names in sequence.

Number one: George Washington.

Number two: John Adams.

Number three: Thomas Jefferson.

And this went on and on, all the way to number thirty-six: Lyndon B. Johnson.

I can remember doing that as if it were yesterday.

Back then people were amazed a four-year-old boy could

so expertly list the presidents in order. It was seen as a sign of my potential. My father, Nunzie, owned a restaurant on Jericho Turnpike, and he liked to bring me in and sit me up on a barstool and challenge customers to give me a number between one and thirty-six.

"Okay," someone would say, "number thirteen."

And I would reply, in my squeaky little boy's voice, "Millard Fillmore."

"How do I know he's right?" they'd ask.

Because there was no Google back then, my father would produce a giant *World Book Encyclopedia* he'd stashed away for just such occasions.

"Give him another number."

"Twenty-nine."

"Warren G. Harding."

"Eight."

"Martin Van Buren."

"Thirty-three."

"Harry S. Truman."

Sometimes my uncle would swing by and spend the day betting customers a dollar that the little mop-haired kid on the barstool could name any president by number, and then he'd buy something off the menu for everyone to share. I would munch on maraschino cherries, and my dad would give me a dime for the jukebox, and I'd play our favorite song, "Winchester Cathedral" by the New Vaudeville Band. And as the song played, I would bask in the obvious pride my father and uncle had in me.

"You watch," my dad would tell patrons. "This kid is gonna be president someday."

My mother liked to tell me the same thing while we sat on the steps and she taught me the names: "Steven, you could grow up to be the president too, just like they did." She said it to me all the time, and I believed her. I believed my father too. I began to think that maybe that was my destiny—to one day be president of the United States.

Many years later, when I was grown-up, I ran into some problems and lost my confidence. I wound up living alone on someone else's property in a cottage that's only three hundred square feet, which is pretty small—about half the size of a school classroom. Sometimes while I sat in my tiny home, I thought about what my parents had told me—that one day I could be president. Only now I wondered why they'd told me that, and why it hadn't happened, and who was to blame, or if anyone was to blame.

But by the time I drove Mrs. Durant into Manhattan, I'd overcome some of the problems in my life, and I was starting on the road back to being happy again. I had my job as a driver, and I had my loyal, regular clients, and I had my beloved collection of records from my father, who gave them to me whenever he replaced the records in his restaurant's jukebox. I had my three older sisters, Annette, Laura, and Nancy, who loved me a lot and sometimes still treated me like the baby brother who needed watching over. I was, mile by mile, making my way back to something like an actual life.

The key to it all, of course, was Oliver.

It was coming up on 7:00 p.m., and I'd been driving for ten hours straight, and I was frazzled and hungry. Driving up the Major Deegan Expressway, heading north out of New York City, I wondered if I should stop at a Chinese restaurant I knew in a strip mall in Scarsdale or if I should keep going, get home, find something to eat in the fridge, and get to bed early so that I'd be ready for my next driving job—a pick-up at the crazy hour of 3:30 a.m. and another drive to JFK Airport.

I was fifty-fifty about stopping for Chinese takeout, and if the traffic had still been bad, I'm sure I wouldn't have bothered to get off the highway. I would have kept driving straight home. But the traffic had finally let up, and I thought about how good a nice plate of chicken fried rice would be. Besides, Oliver surely needed to go to the bathroom by then. He would wait if he had to—he was a good boy that way—but why make him wait? Why not get off at Central Avenue, drive to the strip mall, and let Oliver enjoy the grassy border around the parking lot?

Oliver's Thoughts

I really hope Dad stops soon. I'm trying my best to be good, but I gotta go to the bathroom. Oh, he's getting off the main road! Goody! Maybe he will stop and let me out!

I steered onto Route 100 and got off at exit 5. I wound my way into one of the many strip malls built on the gently sloped hills along Central Avenue, where the town of Yonkers meets the edge of Scarsdale. The parking lot was crowded, but I found a spot. I shut off the engine, picked up Oliver, and took him to the stretch of grass overlooking busy Central Avenue. There was snow on the ground, but it was a peaceful spot, high above the noise of the cars, and Oliver was happy to get to trot around and feel the crisp winter air. He quickly took care of his business, and I picked him back up and put him in my Denali SUV.

"I'll be right back. I'm just gonna run inside for a second," I told him. "You sit tight."

I locked the SUV with my key fob and hustled up the five concrete stairs to the upper parking level, on my way to the China Buffet. There were people coming in and out of the restaurant, more than usual, and it suddenly occurred to me why. *Of course*, I thought, *Valentine's Day. Lovebirds out for a romantic meal.* I smiled as I walked past them. Then I went into the China Buffet to order my takeout dinner.

I wasn't there long. I said hello to the owners, whom I knew, and I remember pausing for a moment to watch the final puzzle on *Wheel of Fortune*, which was playing on a TV in the front of the restaurant. After placing my order, I left to wait in the car until my order was ready. All told, I was in the China Buffet for probably four or five minutes.

Oliver's Thoughts

I think I hear my dad. He's opening the door. Wait, who is this? Huh? This isn't my dad! Why is this man picking me up? Wait! Where is my dad? Put me down! Stee, help!

Back in the parking lot, I dodged mounds of dirty snow and walked down to where I was parked. I unlocked the SUV and swung open the driver-side door. That's when I noticed Oliver wasn't sitting up front, where I thought he would be, waiting for me.

"Oliver, come on up. Let's go," I said, tapping the center console with my fingers. "Come on, boy."

I glanced in the back and didn't see Oliver. It was a large vehicle, with three rows of seats and a cargo area with a small gate. Oliver had to be somewhere back there.

"Oliver, what are you doing? Are you gonna make me come back and find you? Come on, boy."

I opened the rear passenger door, expecting to see Oliver snuggled up on the floor behind the driver's seat. But he wasn't there. Had he wiggled under the seat? I reached down and poked around with my hand. Definitely not enough room under there for Oliver to hide. So where was he?

"Oliver, come on, now," I said, noticing the sudden change in my voice, from normal to something hushed and lower, nearing a whisper. Not alarm, but something.

I climbed into the back and searched the cargo area.

Maybe Oliver had jumped over the gate and settled back there. He never had before, but maybe he did today.

"Oliver, seriously, come on out," I said.

I couldn't find him. I got out and took a deep breath.

Okay, hold on, wait a minute, I thought. *Think about it. Obviously, Oliver is in there somewhere.* I searched the SUV again, then got out again.

Okay, okay. Hold on just a minute. Of course Oliver is in there. Where else would he be?

I looked around the parking lot. People were still coming and going. I got on my knees and looked under the SUV and under other cars. I looked around the grassy area where Oliver had done his business. I didn't call out Oliver's name, because it still seemed ridiculous that Oliver had somehow gotten out of the car. Dogs can't open car doors. But where was he? None of it made sense.

Suddenly, I felt something I recognized.

Panic.

And in that moment, I felt more alone in the world than I had ever felt before.

Slowly, I backed away from the car, as if it were dangerous. I heard myself say the words, "This is not happening," out loud. I slapped myself on the right cheek and said, "Wake up!" I *had* to be sleeping. I had to be dreaming. But I knew I wasn't. My knees felt weak. I tipped forward and had to hold on to the driver-side door to stop from crumbling to the ground. I heard myself breathing hard, and I felt my heart thumping in my chest.

"He's not here," I said. "Oliver's not here."

Oliver's Thoughts

I don't understand. Where is Stee? Where are we going? Who is this man? Why is he driving so fast? I'm scared. I'm scared!

I ran through the parking lot and back to the China Buffet. The man behind the register looked at me with shock.

"What's wrong with you?" he said. "You're as white as a ghost."

"Did I bring my dog in here with me?" I asked. "Did I bring Oliver in? Did you see me with him?"

"No, no dog. Are you okay?"

I ran back outside. Now I was saying something out loud, over and over: "Oliver, where are you? Oliver, where are you, boy?" I felt weak again, so I sat on the concrete steps connecting the upper and lower parking decks. I tried to control my breathing, and I forced myself to think logically.

Okay, Steven, go through the steps. He was with you in the SUV. You definitely brought him with you. You didn't leave him home and get all confused after a long day, right? And then you pulled in here and let him out in the grass and put him back in the SUV and locked the door and went into China Buffet. And when you came back, he wasn't there, he just wasn't there, and . . .

Wait a minute, Steven. Did you lock the door?

I had bought the used Denali just two months earlier.

It didn't feel new to me anymore, but I wasn't quite used to it yet. For one thing, the key fob was strange. The buttons were in different places from what I was used to. Had I pressed the wrong button? Had I thought I was locking the door, when in fact I might have been *unlocking* it? Is that what happened? Could that have happened?

And if I left the SUV unlocked, could it be that someone came by and opened the door and . . . and . . .

I felt an awful, hard knot in my gut, like a punch. It was a mix of shock and rage and fear that comes with losing something that just a moment ago was *right there.* The false, desperate hope that if you just looked hard enough for it, whatever precious thing that was yours would still be yours—would *have* to be yours. Because that is where it belongs, right there with you, right where you left it, and nowhere else.

It seemed like the universe wouldn't dare allow such a terrible thing as losing a dog. It wouldn't dare allow my life to completely change in the blink of an eye. It wouldn't dare allow something so unfair for seemingly no reason at all.

And yet it was happening.

It was real.

I couldn't deny that any longer. Maybe my brain refused to understand what was happening as a way to protect my heart from a terrible reality. But my brain could fool me for only so long. Finally, I understood the truth.

I took out my cell phone and punched in *911.*

"Someone took my dog," I frantically told the dispatcher. "Someone stole Oliver."

Chapter 3

The dispatcher asked me for details. Where was I now, where did it happen, how did it happen?

"I went into the China Buffet, and I came out and my dog was gone," I said, my voice unnaturally loud.

"How long were you in the store, sir?"

"I don't know. Five minutes, tops."

"Could the dog have run away?"

"No, he was in the SUV. The doors were closed! He couldn't have gotten out on his own!"

I was yelling now.

"We'll send a car over, sir."

I looked at the phone in my hand, and I noticed for the first time that I was trembling. I looked out over the cars and trucks cruising on Route 100 and thought of all the drivers heading home or to dinner or to the gym, unaware of how blessed they were that their drives were uneventful or normal or boring. Five minutes ago I had been one of them.

Now I was someone else. But who? I didn't yet know.

I was ten years old when my mother sat me down and told me that she was sick. Cancer, she said.

I didn't fully understand what that meant, but I knew from her voice, and from the heavy gloom that fell over our household, that it was pretty bad news. When she went into the hospital for her third operation, I had a vague understanding there was a chance she might not ever come home.

No one ever explained much of anything about our mother's illness to me. Part of it was to protect me. But I could see with my own eyes how my mother was getting sicker and weaker. I watched her make weekly trips to the hospital and come home with bottles and bottles of pain medicine. Nobody had to tell me anything.

My mother came home from the third operation, and my sisters set up a comfortable reclining chair for her in the den. But she didn't get better. One morning my sister Laura, then twenty-five, led me outside to the front of the house. We sat next to each other on the curb, and Laura put her arm around me.

"Steven, Mom is really sick," she said. "We aren't sure she's going to live much longer. You need to get ready for that. We all do."

I nodded my head to show I understood. Then I stayed there on the curb and cried for a long, long time.

A black-and-white Chevrolet Tahoe with *Greenburgh Police* marked on the side pulled into the parking lot where I was waiting and stopped behind my car. No siren, no strobes—this wasn't that kind of emergency. A uniformed policeman, Officer MacGuire, tall, in his forties, stepped out and opened a small notebook. He asked me for my name.

"Take me through what happened," he said.

I told him the full story: long day, China Buffet, five minutes, Oliver is gone. The officer took notes.

"I don't mean to belittle what you're going through," he said, "but are you sure you had the dog in your car?"

"I understand why you have to ask," I said, "but, yes, I definitely had Oliver with me. Definitely."

"Did you lock the doors?"

"I thought I did, but that's the thing. Maybe I didn't. Maybe I thought I locked the car, but I didn't."

Officer MacGuire asked a few more questions and scribbled something in his notepad. Then we searched the car one more time together. He was being kind and thorough, but even so, I got the feeling the questions and the search were a formality. How many dogs were reported lost or stolen every day? And how many of those reports ever led to finding the dog? *Probably not many*, I thought.

Later, I looked up the statistics. Some two million dogs are lost or stolen every year. Many of those wind up in animal shelters, and of those only 20 percent make it back to their owners. There was no telling what happened to the ones who didn't end up in shelters. But the odds were not on my side.

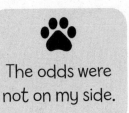

The odds were not on my side.

"I'll look around the parking lot and ask around in the stores," Officer MacGuire said. "What are you going to do?"

"I don't know," I said.

"Are you all right?"

"Honestly? No. I'm in shock."

"Why don't you take some time to settle down before you get back in your car, okay?"

I nodded. That was fine with me. I didn't want to go anywhere. I certainly didn't want to go home.

"I'm going to look around the parking lot too," I said. "I know I probably won't find him. But I'll look anyway."

"That's a good idea," he said. "If someone turns him in or takes him to the pound, we'll contact you right away."

I thanked Officer MacGuire, and we shook hands.

Oliver had now officially been stolen.

The parking lot was emptying out. It had been nearly full when I pulled in; now there were only a handful of cars. I walked around the perimeter, looking everywhere, poking at bushes, calling out Oliver's name. I realized I was going through the motions. No part of me expected to see Oliver in the shadows. One thought pushed its way past all others, much as I tried to fend it off:

I am never going to see Oliver again.

Oliver's Thoughts

Why are we going into this place? Where am I? This isn't my home. It smells different and looks different. Who are these people? Where did my dad go?

I walked around the lot for a full hour. It was past 10:00 p.m., and the last diners were coming out of China Buffet. The night was getting colder, but I didn't care. I held my cell phone in my right hand and squeezed it hard. Finally, I made the call I knew I had to make.

I called my big sister Laura.

"Hi, Steven," she answered. "What's up?"

I couldn't find the words to respond.

"Hello? Steven? What's wrong? Are you all right?"

"I'm fine," I managed to say.

"Is it Oliver?"

"Yes."

"Is he okay?"

"I don't know. He's gone."

"What do you mean, he's gone?"

"He's gone. I had him in the car and I stopped to buy dinner and I came out and he's gone. Somebody stole him."

Laura asked more questions, including the question the police officer asked. Was I sure I had Oliver with me to begin with? Had I searched the SUV thoroughly enough?

Could Oliver have somehow jumped out a window? Was there any other possible explanation?

"Laura, Oliver is gone, and I don't know what to do," I said, my voice nearly strangled by despair.

"Stay right there," Laura said firmly. "I'm on my way." Twenty minutes later, Laura pulled into the lot.

It felt like the cavalry coming.

An Oliver Story

Oliver is a little shy. Some dogs will greet the pizza delivery guy with a big, sloppy kiss at the door, but that's not Oliver. He never makes the first move. When I take Oliver on a walk and a passerby sees him, smiles, and says, "Aw, such a cute pup. You're a good puppy, aren't you?" Oliver will stay close to my leg and look up at me and wait for my opinion of this new person, as if he's saying, *Is this okay? Is this cool? Can I trust this person?* And I will nod and say, "Oliver, go ahead. You can say hi. It's okay." And only then will Oliver go over and wag his tail and let himself be pet on the head.

Chapter 4

*L*aura was the middle of my three older sisters. She was protective of me, as all my sisters were, but Laura and I were probably closer than any of the other siblings. Somehow we'd always managed to live near each other even as adults, and we often got together for dinner or just to let our dogs have a play date. Laura was a dog lover too; that was something else we had in common.

The big difference between us was that I was a bit of a dreamer, a little scattered and messy, while Laura was driven and goal-oriented. I was in awe of her ability to set a target, zero in on it, and blast through all obstacles to reach it. She was analytical, methodical, a problem-solver, and fearless. I'd first seen that side of her during my childhood.

She wasn't scared of tough situations back then, and she is still that way today.

I got up and met Laura on the lower level, near my SUV. She didn't even say hello; she just got right to it.

"Let's search the car again," she said.

I didn't object, and together we inspected every single inch of it, even the tiny nooks and crannies where Oliver couldn't possibly be.

"So he's not here," Laura said.

"That's what I told you. Someone took him."

"And you looked around the parking lot?"

"For an hour. And the police officer did too."

We sat together on the steps and went over everything that happened one more time. Finally, Laura said, "Okay. Do you think you're ready to drive home?"

I hadn't thought of leaving. It hadn't occurred to me. Leaving meant leaving without Oliver, and that didn't seem like an option. It made no sense at all.

Leaving meant leaving without Oliver.

"Yeah, I guess I am," I said.

"You're sleeping at my place tonight," she said.

"Okay, good."

I got in the SUV and followed Laura back to her home in White Plains, fifteen minutes away. It was the worst fifteen minutes of driving I have ever had to endure. Halfway through I looked down at the empty passenger seat and saw Oliver's favorite chew toy, a little yellow rubber duck, lying on the seat. I grabbed it and quickly threw it in the back.

Oliver's Thoughts

They are bringing me water. These people . . . they're nice to me. They are bringing me a toy, but I don't wanna play right now. I just want Stee.

For a moment I wondered if I should have stayed in the parking lot all night, just in case. Then I realized that would have been pointless. If I truly believed Oliver had somehow gotten out of the SUV on his own, I would have spent all night searching the surrounding streets and yards. But I didn't believe that. I may have left the doors unlocked, but I was sure I hadn't left them open. And I hadn't left a window open either. Oliver did not get out of the car on his own. Oliver wasn't lost. Someone had stolen him and taken him God knows where.

At her home, Laura offered me the upstairs guest room. I said I'd rather sleep on the sofa, where I usually slept whenever I crashed at her house. She brought down a pillow and some bedding. I plopped myself on the sofa and half-sat, half-lay there absently.

Laura's tiny brownish-gray poodle, Emma, no bigger than a shoe box, wandered into the living room. Emma's eyes were old and she couldn't see, but she had a system of sliding along the baseboards and softly bumping into walls with her nose, following the sound of humans talking from room to room. Normally, I'd have been thrilled to see Emma, and I'd have scooped her up. Oliver would have been thrilled too, and the two small dogs would have gone together to the backyard to play.

But that night I couldn't bear to pick up Emma and hug her slender, precious frame to my chest. I wanted to, but I couldn't. Emma looked in my direction with her opaque eyes and curled up on the rug at the foot of the sofa. It was as if she knew something was wrong and wanted to console me.

Laura came downstairs, picked her up, and sat with her in a chair so we could talk.

We went over the details of the day. It felt good to have someone to talk to about Oliver. After a while, Laura said she was going to sleep, then turned out the lights and went upstairs. I tucked in the white cotton fitted sheet, stretched out the top sheet, and lay sideways on the sofa, bringing my legs up nearly to my chest. Normally when I slept on Laura's sofa, Oliver would jump up and settle in the space between my arms and legs and sleep there for as long as I did. Oliver didn't sleep in a dog bed. Whatever bed was my bed was also Oliver's bed.

Oliver's Thoughts

I've never slept without Stee. Where are his legs? Where are his arms? Where is he? I'm so tired, but . . . I guess . . . maybe if I fall asleep, I will be in his arms when I wake up.

That night I struggled to keep from thinking where Oliver might be. As I drifted off to sleep, I instinctively reached down to pet Oliver and was startled awake by his absence.

This pattern repeated itself the whole night—short, fitful stretches of sleep ruined by cold bursts of realization. No matter what mental tricks I tried—remembering old New York Mets hitters, replaying World Series games, recalling lyrics from obscure 1950s songs—I simply could not prevent the same terrible questions from racing through my brain.

Where is he? Is he barking? Is he crying? Is he chained up? Is he okay? Is he even alive?

Why isn't Oliver here with me?

An Oliver Story

Oliver starts out sleeping in my bed with me, but when he wants a little more room, he goes over to the chair next to the bed. I'll tuck him in with my scarf, and he'll go to sleep there. The next morning I'll wake up to the sound of his little paws on the floor. He never barks to wake me up, but sometimes he will grunt softly until I get out of bed. Oliver is a good alarm clock that way.

The Search

Day One
February 15

Chapter 5

*T*he first time I ever saw Oliver—and you'll probably say I imagined this—he looked at me like he already knew me. What I mean is, he seemed happy to see me but not surprised. His manner was calm and knowing. He sat there with one ear sticking up and the other flopping down, and he looked at me with his big round eyes and tilted his head, as if he were thinking, *Oh, there you are. What took you so long?*

From the very beginning I felt like we understood each other, as if we were hearing each other's thoughts—as if, somehow, we were able to communicate. Of course, I have no idea how dogs actually think. I'm sure it's not in complete, grammatical sentences. It's more likely they think things like, *Toy. Sleep. Itch. Kibble. Sky.* So, yes, it's possible I was imagining the connection I felt with Oliver that first day or projecting my own thoughts and feelings onto him or reading something into the situation that wasn't there.

But I honestly don't think I was.

Oliver's Thoughts

The first time I saw Stee, I knew he was for me. He brought me into a room and played with me. Boy, did I show off for him! I liked him! I wanted to go home with him. I liked my new puppy friends in the box with all the paper, but I liked Stee better! So I did what puppies do best: I acted cute!

The next thing I knew, some people cut my nails, trimmed my hair, and gave me a bath. Then I saw Stee again, and he held me up, and I heard my name for the first time—*Oliver*. And that's when we went home. We have been together ever since!

Oliver was born on March 9, 2014, and he and I met in a pet store on Memorial Day, just over two months later.

I went there to buy a dog, and I brought along my friend Zoe. While we were looking at the dog who would soon be called Oliver, I asked Zoe if she liked him and what she thought I should name him if I got him. She said the dog looked a little like Chewbacca from *Star Wars*. I told her I didn't know what a Chewbacca was. She looked at me like I was from another planet.

"Steven, you *cannot* let people know you don't know who Chewbacca is," Zoe said impatiently.

After studying the dog's face for a while, Zoe said, "Oliver. He looks like an Oliver." Then she added, "Never Ollie. He's too sophisticated to be an Ollie. Always Oliver."

I held him up and looked him over and said, "Hmm, Oliver. Okay, I like it. It works."

"Of course it works," Zoe replied, again impatiently. "Don't you know I'm really good at naming dogs?"

I brought Oliver home, and we began learning each other's personalities. Over time he got used to how loud I play my records, and I picked up on all his funny little quirks. Like what he does when I ask him, "Oliver, wanna go on a car ride?"

He scampers around the cottage and grabs one of his favorite stuffed animals—maybe his little blue bear, which he loves—and he darts out the front door with the toy in his mouth and stands and waits for me by the car, his little heart beating a mile a minute. After a few rides, when he's brought most of his stuffed animals to the car one by one, I gather them up, bring them back to the cottage, and we start the whole process over.

Funny, silly quirks like that. The things that make you realize, *Gee, I really love that little guy.*

Oliver's Thoughts

I love to play with my dad. I carry out a toy and drop it on the driveway, and he gets all mad! Playfully mad. It's so funny! I do it to him all the time! Sometimes I'll bring the toy into the car. After a while he has to carry them all back inside again. He mumbles under his breath, and I just trot alongside him and chuckle. Stee is so funny when he gets mad at me, because I know he's not really mad at me. I actually think he likes it when I drive him crazy.

The morning after Oliver was taken, I woke up in the darkness of dawn and quietly shuffled through Laura's kitchen and out into her backyard. Laura was asleep upstairs, and I didn't want to wake her. I hoped she'd slept more than I had, which felt like no sleep at all. Outside, the sky was only starting to let in streaky slivers of pink light.

For some reason I went to my SUV in Laura's driveway and searched it yet again. After a few minutes I got out, made a fist, and punched the closed garage door. I didn't even realize I was doing it. The next moment I sat down on the asphalt in a crumpled heap. The shock of the previous night had worn off, and I felt completely empty.

This was the first day I had woken up without a dog with me in twenty-seven years.

Oliver's Thoughts

He's not here. I'm still alone. This is the first time I have ever woken up without Stee. Why is he not with me?

It didn't take long before I started feeling angry too.

Angry at who? I wasn't sure. God, maybe? Yes, that was it—I was angry at God.

"How could You do this?" I half-yelled, looking up at the heavens. "I mean, my dog? The one thing I have in my life? Seriously, God, how could You take my dog?"

People don't really know how they will handle a crisis until they have to handle it. I always assumed that in such a situation I would be calm and strong. Boy, was I mistaken. It turned out I reacted to losing Oliver by drowning in an ocean of self-pity. I am not going to pretend I was calm, cool, and collected, because I want to be completely honest in telling this story. And the honest truth was that I was a wreck. I was full of fear. Oliver was gone. He'd been gone for hours now. He was *long* gone. He could be anywhere or nowhere at all.

Without him, nothing I could think of mattered anymore, not even a little bit. I felt broken and useless.

I looked down and noticed my knuckles were bleeding.

Okay, I thought, *time to pull yourself together, Steven.* I got up, brushed the dirt off my pants, and went back inside Laura's house. I knew Laura would not want me feeling sorry for myself, not even for a moment. It wasn't that she was heartless—she had a bigger heart than anyone I knew. It's that she was fiercely determined. She'd had a long and successful career as an advertising sales executive, and she did it all without a college degree, without even attending college, through sheer willpower and determination.

Laura simply believed that hard work and dedication could make anything come true.

Sure enough, when she came downstairs, she didn't waste a minute with small talk.

"Steven, we have to go back to the strip mall and put up some flyers," she said straightaway.

"I don't want to talk about it," I answered.

"I know you don't want to, but you have to."

"Why do I have to?"

"Because we're going to get Oliver back."

"What?"

"I said we are going to get Oliver back."

"How can you say that?" I asked. "He could be anywhere. He could be dead!"

Laura was as calm as if we were making a shopping list. "We are going to get Oliver back, because we *have* to get him back," she said. "It's as simple as that."

We both knew it was not that simple. But we also knew these were the words I needed to hear at that moment. I needed to have *hope*.

"Steven, please find a photo of Oliver for the flyer," Laura instructed. "Make sure it's clear, and make sure it's really cute. We're going to put his picture *everywhere*."

An Oliver Story

Oliver can't handle when I get mad at him. One time I scolded him for something, and he crawled under my car and stayed there for half an hour. I got on my hands and knees in the driveway and begged him to come out, but he just moved farther away from me. When I finally got him to come out, I hugged him tight and promised I'd never get mad at him again. And I haven't!

Chapter 6

I sat on Laura's sofa and searched through the photos on my cell phone, looking for the best one of Oliver. It wasn't easy. I had a million pictures of him—Oliver running in a field, sitting in the passenger seat, asleep on the bed—but sifting through them made my heart ache. I finally found the one I wanted: a shot of Oliver sitting in the grass and looking up at me, his face a picture of innocence. Laura was at her desk creating the flyer on her computer, and I texted her the photo.

Oliver's Thoughts

Photos? Is that why he always tells me to sit still? And then he points this funny thing at me and says, "Good boy!" when it's all over. Sometimes he even gives me a treat! I always sit still when he points this thing at me. Then he shows me a picture of myself. What funny toys humans have!

"Okay, so how much do you want to offer as a reward for finding Oliver?" she asked.

"I don't know," I said. "Twenty-five hundred dollars?" That was just about all I had in my bank account.

"Fine," Laura said. "Let's start with that. Now, we need to tell people what happened. Think of what you want to say."

Together, it took us thirty minutes to finish the flyer.

CASH REWARD
$2,500
No Questions Asked

Oliver, my beloved dog, was stolen out of my car on Valentine's Day at 1119 Central Park Avenue. I ran into a restaurant, and when I came back, he was gone. If you took him or you know anything about his whereabouts, I beg you to please return him to me. We mean the world to each other, and I know he must be terrified. We love each other very much. If you know anything about my sweet baby, please call me.

Laura began printing out fifty copies of the flyer. I sat on her sofa wondering how else we could spread the word that Oliver was missing. I hit on an idea. Maybe we could get a local TV reporter to do a segment on how Oliver was stolen. I found the phone number for News 12 in Westchester, the local station

I watched, and I called them, but no one answered. Laura and I decided we would keep trying the station throughout the day.

When the flyers finished printing, we got in Laura's car and drove to my rented cottage in Bedford. I had to get a change of clothes and tell the owner of the cottage, Lucy, about Oliver.

Lucy was technically my landlady, but she was much more than that. She was my good friend. Together with her husband, Alan, Lucy owned a five-acre plot of land called Sunny Meadows in the upscale town of Bedford. They lived in the main house and rented out the one-room cottage just off the driveway. Lucy was a former high school social studies teacher and lifelong animal lover who raised goats and rabbits and chickens and had an old white Welsh cross horse named Po (short for Pony Express) and a miniature cow named Anna Belle. Lucy also had a couple of cats, Willie and Georgie, who were in charge of the barn and patrolled for mice. Not long after she and Alan bought the property, they decided to rent out the hundred-year-old cottage. They put an ad online, and I was lucky enough to see it and get the cottage.

I should have been thrilled my first night there, but I wasn't. The photos online didn't show just how small the cottage was. It was fifteen by twenty feet, the size of a walk-in closet in many Bedford homes. It had a kitchenette, a small bathroom, and space for a bed, table, and chair; that was it. Most people would have found it perfect for a single person, but most people's lives weren't as messed up as mine was at the time.

For one thing, the longest relationship of my life had just ended after eight years. For another, a computer-consulting firm

I started went out of business, leaving me with just $1,000 in the bank, a mountain of credit-card debt, and no steady job. All the confidence I once had disappeared, and emotionally I was a wreck. Finding myself in a tiny room on someone else's property seemed to confirm just how far I'd fallen. Basically, I was lost.

The boy who would be president was now the man who had nothing.

Laura and I pulled onto Lucy's property and parked in the driveway between the cottage and the house. Lucy came out to greet us. She was her usual cheerful self, and seeing her smiling made me feel sick. How could I tell her that Oliver, my fur baby she had come to love, was missing? I didn't know how to tell her, so when I got out of the car I just blurted it out.

"Oliver's gone," I said. "Someone stole him."

"Oh no!" Lucy said.

My legs suddenly felt weak again, so I sat down in the grass outside Lucy's house. Lucy sat down with me. She asked what happened, and I told her the story. She tried to console me, but it wasn't much use. It was like I'd become immune to positive thinking. There was simply no combination of words or good wishes that could make me feel less miserable.

And yet, I thought, *people keep trying to help me.*

Suddenly, my sister Laura, who had been on her cell phone, came rushing over.

"Steven, you're going on TV," she said.

"What?"

"I got through to News 12. They're interested. They're going to do a segment on Oliver. Lisa Reyes, the reporter, she's going to meet us outside China Buffet at 3:15 p.m."

I was stunned. Not by the fact that Laura kept calling the station and finally got through and persuaded someone to do a segment—persuading people was like her superpower. No, I was stunned by how hearing the news made me feel. It made me feel . . . what? Good? Hopeful? Knowing that someone believed Oliver's loss was a story worthy of TV, knowing someone *cared* that he was gone, made me feel a little bit less alone in the world.

But just as quickly as that feeling came over me, it went away. I simply couldn't hold on to any positivity for longer than a moment, because it always came back to the terrible truth of my situation.

My best friend in the world was missing.

An Oliver Story

Oliver can read my mind. What I mean is, he knows all my moves. If I'm getting ready to go out and fixing my tie in a mirror, Oliver knows that means I'm going out somewhere. So he'll sit on the bed and watch and wonder, *Is Stee taking me with him? Or am I staying behind?* And all I have to do is look at him in a certain way, and Oliver will know. He'll know if he's going or staying. So like I said, Oliver is a mind reader.

Chapter 7

I went into my cottage and took a shower and changed into some nice clothes. Then Laura drove us back to the strip mall where I'd last seen Oliver. Lucy came along to give us support.

"Are you going to be all right?" Laura asked me as she drove. "I mean, on TV?"

"Yes, I'll be fine," I said. "I'm ready to do this." That was a lie.

We pulled into the parking lot, and I felt a wave of nausea come over me. I had a bottle of water with me, and I drank it all, but I held on to the plastic bottle. I needed something in my hands; otherwise, they would shake.

A few minutes after we got there, a white van with a large satellite dish sticking out the top pulled into the lot. It was marked *News 12 Westchester*. The passenger door opened, and Lisa Reyes hopped out. I recognized her from the nightly 7:00 p.m. newscast. She was the on-scene reporter at car crashes, arrests, and local events. Now she was here to cover the sad story of a stolen dog. *My* stolen dog.

Lisa came over to say hello. She was tall and pretty, with dark hair and a warm, welcoming smile, and she instantly put me at ease. I felt a sudden surge of gratitude for her presence. The last thing I wanted to do was go on television and talk about Oliver, but that was also the *best* thing I could do. And it was only possible because of Lisa's interest. She reached out for a handshake, but I hugged her instead.

The cameraman got in place outside China Buffet, and Lisa told me where to stand. She explained she was going to ask me questions about Oliver and about what happened to him. I took a deep breath and prayed I could keep my composure. Lisa motioned to the cameraman to start filming and turned to face me. I squeezed the empty water bottle in my hand and heard the plastic crinkling.

I took a deep breath and prayed.

Lisa asked me to tell her about Oliver.

"Oliver goes everywhere with me," I said. "We're inseparable. We're best friends. We were together last night, and we stopped here. I went into the restaurant for a minute, and I must have accidentally left the car door unlocked because when I came back out, Oliver was gone."

By the time I finished talking, my eyes were wet with tears.

Lisa talked about how the strip mall had no surveillance cameras, which meant there was basically no evidence to help us in the search, which meant we really needed the public's help in finding Oliver. Lisa referred to the theft as the "Valentine's Day Caper." She turned back to me and asked me what I'd like to say to whoever had Oliver.

"This is breaking me up," I said. "I know Oliver is scared, because he needs me, and I need him. I don't have kids. I'm not married. He's all I've got. Please. *Please*. We need each other."

We need each other.

The cameraman stopped filming. In my hand the water bottle was a crushed ball of plastic.

The News 12 crew took some footage of Laura and me putting up flyers and then drove off. The whole thing took less than half an hour. Laura said we all should go into every store in the strip mall and put up flyers. I didn't think that would work, because I didn't think the store owners would want our desperate flyers cluttering up their walls. Laura would not be deterred. She marched into the China Buffet, and Lucy and I followed her and stood behind her as she approached the hostess and asked if she could put up a flyer.

"Oh my goodness, absolutely, of course you can," the hostess immediately said after hearing about Oliver. "I feel so sorry for you. Please, put up a flyer anywhere you want."

It was the same way in every store we went into. The hair salon. The pet goods store. The deli. Every storeowner listened to our story, told us how sorry they were, and let us put up a flyer. I was taken aback. I hadn't expected such automatic kindness. These people didn't even know me, yet they felt bad for me. They were rooting for me to find Oliver. They cared about my little dog and me. I was exhausted and emotionally drained, but even so, my spirits lifted.

We eventually got in Laura's car and drove back to Lucy's house. While I was there, my sister Nancy called and asked me if I wanted to put Oliver's story on Facebook. I told her I had no interest in that. I wasn't much of a Facebook guy, and I wasn't interested in a bunch of strangers pitying me. Nancy argued that it could be good to have a photo of Oliver on Facebook. I told her I rarely ever went on Facebook anyway, so what was the point?

"What is there to lose?" Nancy said. "If you don't want to post it, I'll post it for you on my page. I'm always on Facebook."

"If you want to do it, be my guest," I finally said. "Knock yourself out."

I had no idea what Nancy posted, but a short while later she told me the story had already been shared five times.

"No, wait, eight shares," she said. "Ten shares!"

I didn't know what that meant. Was ten shares good? Was it a lot? I had no idea and didn't much care. I just didn't see how a bunch of strangers on the internet could ever play a part in finding Oliver. What help could they possibly be?

While I was sitting in Lucy's living room, staring ahead and thinking angry thoughts, Lucy's husband, Alan, came down the stairs and sat next to me. To be honest, I wasn't thrilled to see him. I wanted to be alone.

Alan is a sweet and lovely man, one of the very nicest people

I've ever known, but also a little shy and reserved. He doesn't talk all that much; it's almost as if he's decided to let Lucy do all the talking for them. We weren't exactly close, certainly not as close as Lucy and I had become. We'd never had a real, heart-to-heart conversation about anything, but we got along just fine. Alan leaned toward me and looked at me with the same sad-eyed expression I had already grown tired of.

"Lucy told me what happened," Alan said. "I'm so sorry."

"Thanks," I said.

Alan paused and took a deep, loud breath.

"You know, we don't really know why things happen in life," he said.

Oh, boy, I thought. *Here we go. I don't want to have a talk. I just want to be alone.*

"Oliver was taken from you," Alan said. "But we don't know the reason he was taken."

"What do you mean?"

"You went into that restaurant, but if you hadn't, a whole different set of things could have happened. Maybe Oliver getting stolen protected you from something even worse."

I was dumbstruck. I'd never heard Alan talk like this. I'd barely heard him talk at all. Maybe we'd discuss the weather or the goats or what we had for breakfast. Where was this coming from?

"Steven," Alan said, leaning in closer, "we have to trust that when something happens, *it happens for a reason.* Maybe your life was saved last night. We just don't know."

With that, Alan got up and went back upstairs.

Much later, when I told Lucy what Alan had said to me in one of my darkest moments, she was sure he couldn't possibly have said it.

"He doesn't talk like that," she said. "Alan doesn't go deep like that."

And yet he had, and what's even crazier is that what he said somehow got through my thick brick wall of negativity.

Along with the unexpected kindness of the restaurant and shop owners at the strip mall, Alan's strange little speech was the start of my journey to understanding that losing Oliver was not, as I had thought, the end of something. It was just the beginning.

An Oliver Story

I live on a farm, where there are lots of animals—goats and rabbits and a horse and a miniature cow. Oliver gets along pretty well with them all. Oliver likes it when I grab a loaf of bread off the top of my fridge and go feed the goats. He follows along and gets in line and waits for his turn. One time he got a little too close to the goats, and one of them put its head down and gave him a good little shove. Oliver got the message pretty quickly. Now he never, ever tries to cut in line.

Chapter 8

That night I lay awake in bed and thought about Oliver. I wondered where he was, how he was, who took him, and how scared he was. These were all questions without any answers, so to make myself feel better I tried to put myself in Oliver's head.

I knew Oliver was an especially gentle and sensitive dog. With other small dogs I've had, I was able to horse around with them, roll in the grass and tussle and frolic, without worrying too much. They were sturdy. But Oliver was different. There was something a little fragile about him.

"He's a baby," one friend told me when I got him. "You have to be easy with him. He's your little angel."

But whoever had Oliver now didn't know this about him. They had no idea how sensitive he was. And even if they knew, would they care? Would they show any concern for Oliver's welfare? Or had they just stolen him for kicks?

The one thing I kept telling myself, as I lay in the dark grasping for any assurance, was, *Oliver is smart. He's a very smart dog. That is in our favor.* Oliver trained very quickly, knew his toys by name, and knew how to look out for himself. He was playful and friendly, and he had a big, open heart, but he also knew when to back off and seek safety. I never put him on a leash on Lucy's property, because he never wandered away or got lost. He had the instinct to stay out of trouble.

Which matters, I told myself, *because he's in a situation now where he needs to be smart.*

As soon as the door to my SUV opened and a strange pair of arms reached in to take him, Oliver would have known something was wrong. *This is not my dad*, he would have thought. *This is not good.* But he wouldn't have fought his abductor; he was too small and sweet to do that. He wasn't aggressive, and he wasn't a biter; he was a retreater. He wasn't even a growler. I've had dogs who growl when someone approaches them too abruptly or a kid rushes over and startles them, but not Oliver. Oliver just runs away. Maybe he'll growl a little bit when I tease him by keeping a toy away from him, but it isn't really much of a growl. It's more adorable than menacing.

So he wouldn't have growled or snipped or barked. He would have played it cool. Yes, that's what Oliver would have done as he was carried away from the car and away from me. He would have swallowed his fear and bewilderment, and he would have played along.

Okay, I thought, *so now Oliver is out of the SUV and into someone else's car. Why did they take him? Why did this person steal Oliver?* Maybe if I understood why they took him, I'd have a better chance at figuring out where he was. *Well, they stole him so they could sell him,* I figured.

Little dogs go for lots of money in pet stores, and someone could probably get a few hundred dollars for Oliver. Or they might have taken him to keep him as their own. He was certainly cute and irresistible. Either motive was okay with me, because they both required that Oliver be fed and cared for. Any other motives I refused to even consider. I had to believe that whoever took Oliver had an interest in keeping him safe and sound.

I began to think through what Oliver's journey must have been like.

So there is Oliver, in the passenger seat of a stranger's car, huddled in a little ball against the back of the seat, as far away from his abductor as he can get. *Who is this guy?* he would think. *Where am I going? Where is my dad?* He would wonder all these things, but he wouldn't panic. How could I be so sure? Because *I* knew that *Oliver* knew that I would stop at nothing to get him back, and so all Oliver had to do was bide his time and play it cool.

All Oliver had to do was bide his time and play it cool.

I'll do what I'm told. I'll sit where they put me. I won't make noise. If they want to pet me, I'll let them pet me. And in time, Dad will come and get me. And then we'll go back to how it was.

Oliver's Thoughts

Stee taught me a long time ago how to behave. Us dogs used to live in packs, and the alphas were the leaders. These people must be my new leaders. I don't get it, but I'll act like my dad told me to. They seem to like me, so I'll just like them back. But if I ever get the chance, I'm getting out of here. I'll have to go find Stee myself.

Yes, I was sure of it. This was how Oliver would handle getting stolen. And when I focused on this, I felt better, because—though I didn't dare vocalize it in any way—I understood deep down that if Oliver did indeed play it cool and play it smart, as I knew he would, then even if I *didn't* get him back, he would be okay. Because whoever took him would fall in love with him, just as I had, and they would take care of him and protect him from harm. And so Oliver would be okay—heartbroken, as I would be—but physically safe, and surely loved by someone else. And that, I understood on some deep level, would not be the worst thing that could happen, at least not for Oliver.

Which, in the middle of the dark and sleepless night, was just about the only comfort I could find.

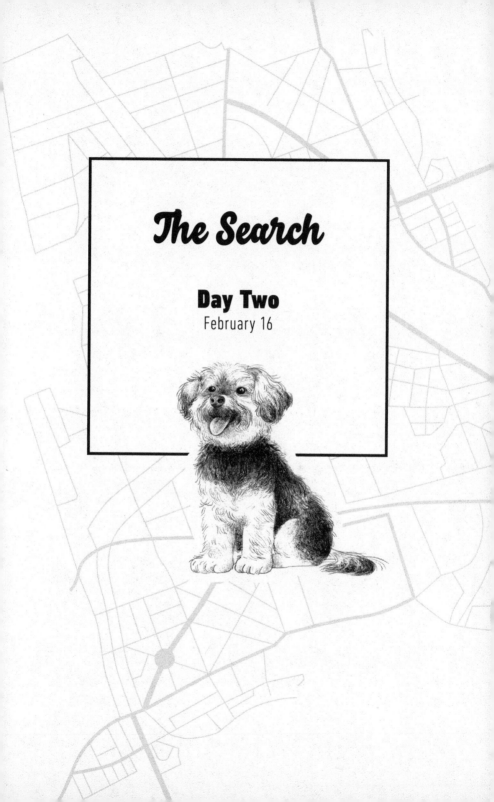

The Search

Day Two
February 16

I woke up in a bad mood. Never mind that the day before we felt like we'd scored a little victory by getting our story on News 12. But then I began to think, *Why isn't the phone ringing? Why hasn't Oliver already been found? Has anybody even seen the news report?* And in the harsh light of day, my little scraps of hope seemed pretty measly.

My sister Nancy called and said she was driving up from Brooklyn, where she lived, to spend the day with Laura and me and help in any way she could.

"Nancy, you don't have to do that," I said.

"Steven, I'm coming."

I also got a call from an old friend, Eric Weinstein. Eric and I knew each other from back in Huntington Station, where we'd attended junior high and Walt Whitman High School together. Eric had a paper route in town when we were kids, and he helped me get one too—my very first job.

Early Sunday mornings we'd meet in his garage and sort through a stack of thick Sunday *Newsdays*. We'd stuff our canvas bags full of them, sling the bags over the handlebars of our bikes, and ride off on our routes. Eric had one of those bikes with huge handlebars, so the heavy Sunday papers didn't seem to be much of a problem for him. My bike had regular handlebars, and the Sunday papers weighed me down so much I felt like I was pedaling through mud.

Now, many years later, Eric was calling because I'd left him a message that Oliver was gone, and he was insisting that he would come up from Amityville, Long Island—a long sixty-mile drive—to be with me and help me look for Oliver.

"Eric, don't be crazy. You don't have to come," I said.

"Steven, you're my friend," he said. "I'm coming." Our little search party was starting to grow.

The last few days of my mother's illness were the worst. One morning paramedics came to our house and rushed my mother to Memorial Sloan Kettering Hospital in New York City. I saw her one last time that day. I stood by her bed in her hospital room, with my father on the other side of the bed, as she spoke with us.

"Take care of Steven," she told my father. "He is a special boy. Be good to him."

My dad looked at me and nodded. It was his way of telling me he would do his best to honor my mother's wish. And though I knew there would be hard times ahead, I believed he meant it. My father was a good man. But he also had a mean side.

Then my mother told me she would always be there with me, and for me, but just in a different way than I was used to.

I believed her too. She passed away three days later.

Up until the moment she passed, I later realized, I'd thought of myself as special. I was loved and championed by my parents, and especially by my mother, and I felt like I had been chosen for something great in life. Grown-ups thought I was smart and funny and charming, and I felt comfortable in my skin. I had confidence to spare. I could hardly wait for my future to unfold.

But when my mother died, that all changed. The feeling of being special went away. The confidence and optimism disappeared, replaced by feelings of loss and abandonment. I was no longer comfortable in my own skin.

I felt like I had been chosen for something great in life.

I wouldn't feel comfortable again for a long, long time.

Chapter 10

*L*ater that morning, Nancy showed up at Laura's house. When I was a kid, Nancy and I had not been all that close. She was only five years older than me, but that was enough of a gap to keep us from being buddies. Basically, I was a pest who couldn't help annoying her and her girlfriends. Whenever they'd come over to our house and hang out in Nancy's bedroom, I'd attach my suction-cup tape recorder to the telephone in the living room and try to tape their calls. I had to pick up the receiver very delicately so they wouldn't hear me tinkering with it, but they always did. And I'd hear Nancy scream, "Steven, stop trying to tape us!"

When we got older, though, Nancy and I bonded over the shared challenge of dealing with our unpredictable dad. When I asked my father to teach me to drive, he couldn't help but yell and scream at me if I did something wrong, so Nancy took over and taught me how to drive her really cool orange 1973 Volkswagen Bug. Sometimes she'd even let me borrow the Bug so I could drive my friends around in it.

When Nancy came into Laura's house, she came over and gave me a big, long hug. I melted into it. She told me she was praying for me, and so were her husband, John, and her kids, Christian and Jena. I thanked her and told her it felt really good to have her there.

Not much later, my friend Eric also showed up. Eric is smart and quick-witted, and he knows a million jokes. Give him a topic—eating, sleeping, dancing—and he'll have a joke for it. I swear, he could have been a professional stand-up comic. When I saw him walk through Laura's front door, I felt the tension drain from my body. He was *exactly* the person I needed to have around at that moment.

He was exactly the person I needed to have around at that moment.

Laura printed out fifty more flyers, and she and Nancy drove to Scarsdale to put them up in the area where Oliver had been stolen—on shop windows, telephone poles, bulletin boards, everywhere they could. Eric and I were in charge of calling all the veterinarians and animal hospitals in the area to ask about Oliver, let them know he had been stolen, and give them a description in case anyone brought him in. Eric and I got in his car to drive around while I made the calls.

"Hey, does Oliver have a chip?" Eric asked. "You know, one of those implanted chip things?"

"I don't know. I can't find his paperwork."

"So call the place where you got him. They'll know."

I called the pet store in Huntington where I bought Oliver, and sure enough, they told me he did have an implanted identification chip. That meant a veterinarian could scan the chip and pull up the dog's medical information and the names of its owners. But how was that going to help me find Oliver? Those chips weren't homing devices. They couldn't pinpoint his location. I wasn't sure what good Oliver's chip would do.

"Call the chip company," the man at the pet store told me. "They'll put an alert on him. If he is brought into any vet or shelter, they will run a scan on the dog, and an alarm will sound to let them know the dog is lost or stolen."

So that's what I did. I had the chip manufacturer put an alert on Oliver. It felt like a real accomplishment. We were covering the bases. Working all angles. It felt good.

But only for a moment, before I got all gloomy again.

Oliver's Thoughts

I hope my dad didn't forget about me. I know he must be trying to find me. I don't mind playing it cool for these people, but I really miss Stee right now. I thought it was always going to be Stee and me forever.

After driving around and making calls for two hours, Eric pulled us into a Dunkin Donuts. We ordered coffee and sat at a table by the window. I was silent and stared into the dark brown pool in my cup. Eric looked at me with concern.

"Steven, I have to say, I'm worried about you," he said. "I watched you when you were looking out the car window, and it scared me. You were gone. You weren't even there. You're not here now. I've never seen you this bad, Steven, not even when your mom died."

I felt like I was all alone.

I didn't say anything. What was there to say? I was in a bad way, and I knew it. Eric had seen me at other low points in my life, but this was different. Losing Oliver set off a chain reaction of anger and self-pity that upended the very foundation of my life. The unfairness of it all was staggering. I felt like I was all alone in my overwhelming grief and sorrow.

"I'll be okay," was the best response I could muster. We drove back to Laura's house without saying much.

Laura and Nancy were back from putting up flyers. Nancy came over with a smile on her face.

"The Oliver Facebook post is up to three hundred shares!" she said.

"Is that good?" I asked.

"It's unheard of," Nancy said. "That's a lot of people following a little local story. And look at what they're saying."

Nancy showed me some of the comments below the post. I'd told her that I didn't want sympathy from strangers, but these comments went beyond sympathy.

"I don't even know you personally, but I am home right now with my dog, and I am crying my eyes out for you," read one.

"This breaks my heart," read another. "Please tell Steven I am saying my prayers that he finds Oliver soon."

"I can't stop crying. Steven, please let me know if there's anything I can do to help you get Oliver back."

There were dozens and dozens of comments just like these. Reading them took my breath away, and I had to sit down. These weren't just random well-wishers tossing off kind comments. These were people speaking from their hearts and sharing their own distress over what happened. These were people who were crying, just like I was. They didn't know Oliver or me, yet they experienced real pain and sadness over our separation.

These were people speaking from their hearts.

Suddenly, losing Oliver didn't feel like it was my own private agony. Our story had touched the hearts of all these people, almost as if it had happened to them. How was this possible? Why did people care so much about some guy and his dog? What was happening?

And then I thought, *Maybe I'm not as alone in this thing as I think I am.*

Oliver's Thoughts

Stee is a good person. I know that because people always smile when they talk to him. I bet his friends and family are helping him. I hope they are. I don't want my dad to feel alone right now.

I changed my mind about the Facebook post and gave Nancy some new pictures of Oliver to put up. I didn't want to post anything myself, but I was okay with Nancy keeping the story current and sharing any news with followers. I could see that all of us—Nancy, Laura, Eric, me—felt energized by the reaction on Facebook. But I could also tell that, though I was inspired by the support, I was less energized than the others. Losing Oliver was always going to be more personal to me because, after all, he was my dog. So I didn't get quite as excited by small bits of progress as the rest of our little team. That was just the way it was going to be, I figured.

It was getting late, and I walked Eric to his car. Before he got in, he turned to me and gave me an enormous hug.

Then he stepped back and looked at me.

"Steven, don't you see who you are?" he asked. "You're George Bailey!"

"What are you talking about?"

"George Bailey. From *It's a Wonderful Life.*"

I knew the movie he was talking about. It's a movie about a man who was going through some bad things and convinced himself that his life didn't have any meaning. Then an angel came to see him and showed him what life would have been like if he'd never been born. George got to see how important he had been to so many people, and how he had changed their lives in ways he didn't realize. He was much more loved and appreciated than he could have imagined.

"Maybe that's you, Steven," Eric said. "Maybe you're George Bailey, and you don't even know it!"

I thought about it for a moment. I couldn't deny that people were rallying to my side. My family. My friends. My clients. The strip mall shop owners. Three hundred strangers on Facebook. People were stepping forward and giving me advice and support and encouragement and, yes, love.

> People were giving me advice and support and encouragement and, yes, love.

"Steven, you're a good guy, and people love you," Eric went on. "Maybe you really needed to see just how much people love you. Maybe that's why Oliver was taken, so you could see it. Steven, I believe you're going to get Oliver back. But this whole thing—this is about your *journey*, man."

I hugged Eric and watched him drive away. When I went back inside Laura's house, Nancy rushed over again.

"We're up to five hundred shares, Steven!"

By the next morning the number of people following our story was over a thousand.

An Oliver Story

I miss Oliver when he's not around. Even worse is that I know he misses me too. After our walks he doesn't follow me into the cottage. Instead, he stays outside next to the car because he thinks I'm going somewhere and wants me to take him with me. And so, every time, I have to explain it to him: "Daddy's got to go out. Daddy's got to go to work. I'm gonna leave the TV on, and you need to be a good boy, okay? Don't worry, Daddy will be back soon." What Oliver doesn't realize is that I'm probably sadder than he is that I'm leaving.

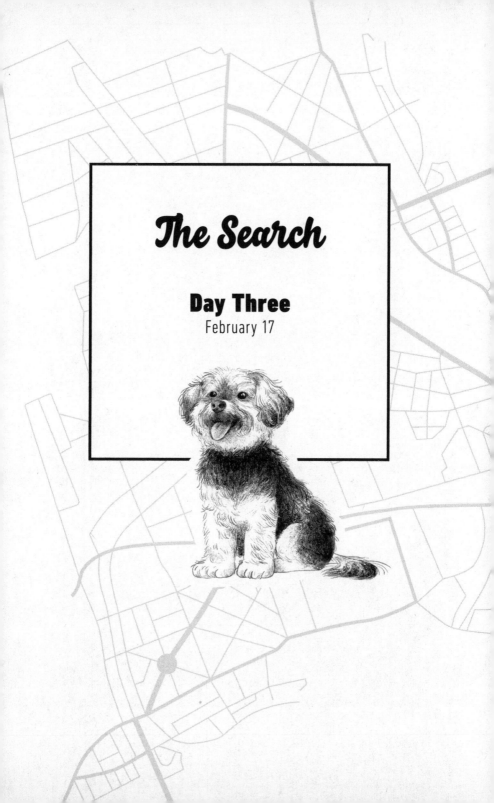

The Search

Day Three
February 17

Chapter 11

I knew what Eric meant about me being George Bailey, but another long night of no sleep wiped away any good feelings I had from his visit. In the past two days, I hadn't received a single bit of information about Oliver's whereabouts. Nothing. Zero. No clues or leads at all. I walked around feeling like I might burst into tears at any moment.

Awake, I was restless and miserable; asleep, I was plagued by nightmares. I decided I needed to disrupt the pattern, if only for a short while. While my sisters Laura and Nancy went back to Scarsdale to post more flyers, I took a quick break from searching for Oliver and went to my local gym.

But as soon as I walked into my gym, I knew I wouldn't be able to work out. I had no energy, and my body felt like it was made of lead. There was no way I'd be able to summon the enthusiasm I needed for the workout. That's when I realized that losing Oliver wasn't just about losing my dog.

Whoever took Oliver took away my life.

It was true. Everything that I'd loved about my life before—my family, my friends, working out, eating at restaurants, going for walks, being with Oliver—were now things I could no longer enjoy. How could I enjoy eating a nice meal when I knew that Oliver was out there somewhere, waiting for me to find him? How could I do *anything* without feeling guilty and empty? The answer was, I couldn't. Losing Oliver had destroyed my spirit. It had sapped me of all purpose and desire. It was like stripping the engine out of a car—all that's left is a useless shell.

> How could I do anything without feeling guilty and empty? The answer was, I couldn't.

"So I guess this is it," I said aloud on my way out of the gym. "This is my life now. Go to work, come home, try to sleep. If I don't get Oliver back, this will be my life."

Then I had another thought: *Maybe my father was right.*

Whenever my father got into one of his bad moods, he would tell us children that we would have a hard time succeeding in life. He didn't mean what he was saying; he just couldn't help himself. So he'd tell us that no matter what good things happened to us, something bad was always going to be right around the corner, waiting to drag us down.

"It's the Carino way," he'd say, using our last name. Outside the gym, I thought back to when he'd say that.

You know what, Dad? I thought. *I guess you were right. I guess this is the Carino way.*

When I was little, my mother and older sisters protected me from my father's bad moods. But after my mother passed away and my sisters got older and moved on with their own lives, my father and I were basically stuck with each other. Like I said, my father was a good man, and he was often a really great father. He was kind and thoughtful and gentle, and he made it clear to us that he loved his children.

But then the bad moods would come, and my father would become a different person.

When my older brother, Frankie, came home one day with a new car he worked very hard to buy, my father couldn't stop himself from mocking him.

"You just threw away all your money," he told Frankie. "That's the worst car you could have bought."

Watching Frankie's face drop and his shoulders slump was painful. I felt so bad for him. There was no use arguing with my father; that would only make it worse. All you could do was accept the humiliation and walk away defeated.

When I got to Walt Whitman High School, I found a job

working at the Mobil gas station on Jericho Turnpike. It felt like a real, adult job, and I was proud and delighted to have it, despite how dirty I'd be at the end of my shift. Then I told my father about it.

"That is the worst place any person can ever work," he said. "That's a terrible job. Why would you ever work there?"

In time, I learned not to share any of my accomplishments with my father. If I got the high score in pinball with my friends, I kept it to myself. If I aced a math quiz, I stuffed the test in my book bag and forgot about it. This way, my father wouldn't be able to knock me down with insults. All I had to do was conceal the best and happiest moments of my life, and I'd be fine. I realized it was safer to be a total nobody in my father's eyes.

> I lost interest in having any achievements at all.

The consequence of that strategy, though, was that eventually I lost interest in having any achievements at all. In Little League I begged the coach not to put me in the games, and finally I quit altogether. In high school I was a really good bowler, but when I tried out for the team, I purposefully choked in the final two frames so I wouldn't make the squad. I felt like no matter what I did, it wouldn't be good enough for my father, so why even bother? I knew what I needed to do to avoid getting yelled at by my father, and what I needed to do was nothing.

Unfortunately, I began to go through life with no passion

or excitement, since there seemed to be no reward for getting excited about anything. A pattern developed. In my life I would take one step forward and two steps back. This was the message my father instilled in us—that a Carino would never amount to anything. That a Carino might get close to succeeding but then find some way to mess it up, because that's just what a Carino did. One step forward, two steps back—that was the Carino way.

That was why, when I lost Oliver, part of me wasn't even surprised. *Of course Oliver is gone!* I thought. *Why wouldn't he be? Get something good and mess it up! That's the Carino way!*

That evening, when I was back at Laura's house, Laura got a call on her cell phone. I could tell she knew the person and was surprised to hear from them. After a minute or two, she came over and gave me the phone.

"Steven, it's Uncle Pat," she said.

"Uncle Pat? What's he calling for?"

"He heard about Oliver."

Uncle Pat is my mother's brother, and he lives in Delaware with his wife, Rita. Laura and I had visited him there a year earlier, but after that we hadn't talked at all. We had fallen out of touch. So I was as surprised as Laura to hear from him now.

"Steven, I'm so sorry about Oliver," Uncle Pat said. "I saw it on Nancy's Facebook page, and it broke my heart. I'm sitting here now with my two little babies on my belly, and I know how much Oliver means to you. And I am just so sorry."

Uncle Pat's two babies were a pair of adorable Miniature Pinschers both he and Rita loved dearly.

"Steven, you have to get Oliver back," he went on.

"We're working on it, Uncle Pat," I said.

"What's the reward amount?"

I told him we were offering $2,500.

"Make it $5,000," Pat said. "I'll send you a check."

"Uncle Pat, you don't have to do that."

Do whatever you have to do to get back that dog.

"Steven, let me do it. Double the reward. Then do whatever you have to do to get back that dog. You've had more than your share of troubles in your life, and I'd feel guilty if I didn't do something to help you out."

The next morning Nancy updated her Facebook post and changed the reward to $5,000.

"NO QUESTIONS ASKED," she wrote in the post in all caps. "We are up to 3,700 shares. Amazing! Please, keep sharing. Maybe your share will be the one that brings Oliver home."

How about that? I thought. *Another unexpected act of kindness and compassion from someone who cares about me.*

Maybe Eric had been right. Maybe I was George Bailey after all.

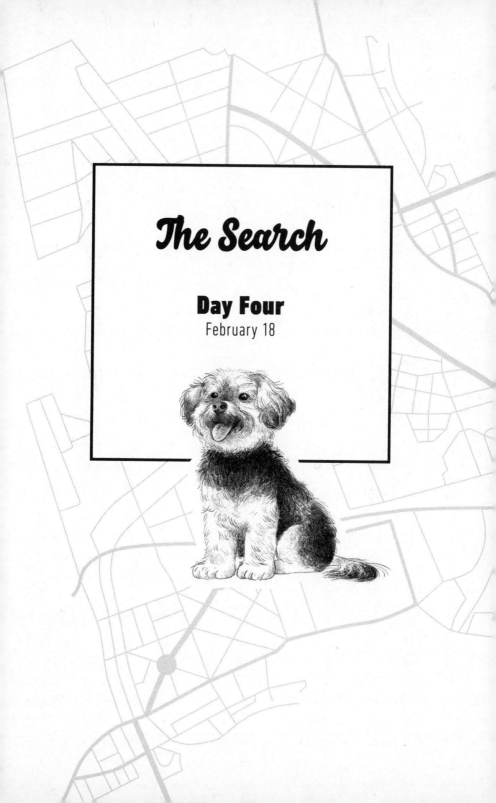

The Search

Day Four
February 18

Chapter 12

The day after Oliver disappeared, someone who was trying to be helpful told me they hoped I'd find him in the next three days.

"After three days," they said, "the odds of finding him get really terrible."

I thought about that when I woke up on my fourth day without Oliver. Not only did I not have him; I didn't have the slightest idea where he was or what might have happened to him. I'd received a few texts from friends and colleagues who saw the News 12 TV report, but none from anyone who had information about Oliver. The case of the stolen dog was stone cold.

I drove to the local Kinko's in White Plains and ran off one hundred copies of the flyer, updated with the new reward.

"Sorry to hear about your dog," the guy behind the counter said.

"Oh, thanks."

"I hope you get him back. I'm pulling for you."

I smiled and put him on the list of positive encounters.

Back at Laura's house, my sister and I sat down and planned the day. Laura would take the flyers to Scarsdale and hand one to everybody who came into the China Buffet.

"Steven, do you have any cute pictures or videos of Oliver we could send to Lisa Reyes at News 12?" Laura asked.

"Lemme look," I said.

On my phone I found a video of Oliver getting chased around Lucy's driveway by her cat. It was cute and funny, though I couldn't bear to watch it all the way through.

"How's this?" I asked.

"Perfect," Laura said. "This shows how precious Oliver's life was on the farm with you. I'll send it to Lisa. Maybe she'll run an update on Oliver."

Oliver's Thoughts

I miss the farm and all my friends. I don't see any grass where I am. I used to like to run in the grass and see the goats and chickens. I remember when I was little, Willy the cat would chase me under the cars. Now I chase Willy! At least I used to. I wonder if I'll ever see my friends again.

A call came in on my cell, and I looked at the number.

It wasn't familiar. Could it possibly be an Oliver sighting? "Hi. Who is this?" I asked.

The answer came in a child's voice. A child who was crying. "I'm Helen," she said. "Are you Steven?"

"Yes, I'm Steven."

"I got your number from a poster. I just wanted to tell you that I am so sad you can't find Oliver. I love my own dog so much, and I can't imagine someone taking him. I want to send you a picture of my dog so you'll feel better."

She was crying and sniffling through the whole call. I was disappointed it wasn't a tip, but I was also overwhelmed by Helen's kind and innocent heart.

"Thank you, Helen," I said. "And I'll send you a picture of Oliver too."

"Okay, that would be great. I really want you to find him. I'm, like, praying you find him really soon."

"Me too," I said. "Me too."

A few seconds later I got Helen's text. She sent me a photo of her with a beautiful white Labrador. She looked so happy in the photo, and so did the Lab. I put my phone away.

I'd lost enthusiasm for everything in my life, but that didn't mean I could suddenly do nothing. For example, I had to keep working as a driver, because I couldn't afford to be out of a job. That fourth day without Oliver, I had three different driving jobs to do—two were taking clients to an airport, and the last one was driving the niece of a regular client to her college in southern Massachusetts.

Somehow I made it through the first two drives without crying in front of my clients. Finally, I pulled into the driveway of one of my regular clients in Bedford, Bryce, for the last job of the day. I got there thirty minutes early, so I had some time to sit and think. From the SUV I could see a magnificent clock that stood in the meadow across from my client's home, on the corner of two roads. It was called the Sutton Clock Tower, and it was maintained by the Bedford Historical Society. A guy named James F. Sutton built the clock in the late 1880s because his wife, Florence, was homesick for the sound of church bells. The bell weighed 550 pounds and was hung in an elegant brick tower. Each year a group of twelve families from the area become the official Clock Winders who took turns winding it once a month.

I loved the Sutton Clock Tower. I drove by it often, and I always paused to appreciate how beautiful it is. While I was admiring it from my car, it occurred to me that, though I'd driven past it probably a hundred times, I'd never once heard it chime. Not a single time. I was sure the sound of the bell would only make me love the old clock more.

At 7:30, I knocked on Bryce's front door. He led me into the kitchen, and his niece Isabela, whom I'd never met, met us there. She had long reddish hair and a friendly demeanor.

"I heard about Oliver," Bryce said. "I'm so sorry."

"What?" Isabela said. "Who's Oliver?"

Bryce explained how he'd seen the News 12 report and how my dog had been stolen four days earlier. Isabela cringed. I could tell she felt bad for me, which made me feel really bad about the whole thing.

"I'm so sorry," she said. "Are you okay to drive?"

"I'm fine," I said. "It's good for me to drive. It takes my mind off the whole Oliver situation."

Bryce kindly suggested that we take his Jeep for the two-hour drive so I could spare my car the mileage. We climbed into the Jeep, and Isabela asked if she could sit in the front passenger seat, which almost none of my clients do. I said yes, of course she could, and having her up front put us both a little more at ease. Even so, Isabela seemed unsure of what to say to me as we began the eighty-mile drive up I-684, on the way to Route 22 and the town of Great Barrington, Massachusetts. A light snow began to fall, and I flicked on my windshield wipers. For fifteen minutes, we drove in silence.

Finally, Isabela asked, "Hey, do you mind if we put some music on?" She held up her phone so I could connect it to the car stereo. Suddenly, I froze. The truth was, I hadn't listened to any music since Oliver disappeared. I'd tried to, but I found I couldn't bear it. I was very passionate about music, and I used to play my favorite songs in my cottage with Oliver in my lap, listening as

Suddenly, I froze.

I sang along. Now I was afraid that if I heard any of my favorite songs on Isabela's playlist, it would trigger the overwhelming sadness and anger that was always just beneath the surface, and I'd start to cry.

Oliver's Thoughts

I miss hearing my dad's music. He loves music! I know two of his favorite singers by name: Elvis Presley and Sam Cooke. Music and Stee and breakfast together every morning. I miss that so much.

Then I thought, *Wait. Isabela is eighteen years old. What are the chances she likes the same music I do? After all, I'm stuck in the 1950s and '60s. I love Elvis Presley! Surely Isabela listens to music that is slightly more modern than that.*

"Of course," I said, activating the Bluetooth that connected Isabela's phone to the car. I held my breath while the first song cued up. Finally, it came on.

It was a song by the Eagles.

Okay, I thought. *The Eagles are a little old for an eighteen-year-old, but still, you're okay, Steven. You're safe with the Eagles.*

The next song was by the Rolling Stones. The one after that was by the Beatles. Two bands from the 1960s.

Now we're getting kind of close to the danger line, I thought. *What if Elvis is next? You won't be able to handle it if she plays Elvis.*

"Wow, you have great taste in music," I said.

"Thanks! I love the older stuff because it's what my father listens to."

Oh, great.

The next song was "Burning Love."

By Elvis Presley.

"You like Elvis?" I asked, trying to keep my emotions in check.

"Oh, I *love* Elvis," she said.

"Yeah, me too. He's my favorite ever. It's just . . . I haven't been able to listen to Elvis since Oliver disappeared."

After a pause, Isabela said, "Do you want me to turn it off? We can turn it off."

"No, leave it. That's okay. I can listen to this. I'm okay."

The next two songs were by Elvis too. The last one was called "Always on My Mind." When Elvis sang, "Maybe I never told you I'm so happy that you're mine," I felt myself begin to shake. I couldn't stop it. The emotion in Elvis's voice tore away at me. Ripped me to pieces. Suddenly I was crying, then gasping for breath. Slowly, I pulled the car over to the side of the road.

"I'm sorry," I said. "I just . . . I can't listen to this. It's too hard. I'm so sorry."

I felt Isabela put her hand on my shoulder. She didn't say anything. She just kept her hand there while I cried. After a minute, she handed me a tissue. I felt like I needed to explain why I was so emotional.

"It's just . . . it's just that I don't know if . . ." I searched and struggled for the right words. "It's just that I don't know if I told him I loved him that day."

"Oliver knows that you love him," Isabela said.

"Yeah, but I don't know if I *told* him. What if I didn't tell him? I didn't know I would never see him again."

We fell into a silence, and I asked if it was okay if we went to a gas station to get some coffee. I knew I needed to pull myself together. The coffee helped, and we got back on the road. The snow had picked up but not to the point where it was a problem. In fact, it gave the night a wonderful winter feel, which, under normal circumstances, I'd have enjoyed.

"You really love your dog," Isabela said.

It was as if she sensed I needed to talk to someone, which was true—I did. Since Oliver's disappearance, I really hadn't talked about Oliver with anyone, except for my brief conversation with the TV reporter Lisa Reyes. Every moment of every day had been devoted to finding Oliver, not to remembering what he was like or what was special about him. Somehow Isabela knew I needed to talk about my boy.

"I do," I replied. "I really do love him. And I'm trying to understand why this happened, you know? To understand why he was taken from me."

"You know, you might get him back. Just because he was taken doesn't mean he was taken forever."

"It's been four days, and we're nowhere," I said. "I'm starting to think God has some lesson He needs to teach me, and I just wish He didn't have to take my dog to show me what it is."

And *just then*, without Isabela saying a word, with the soft snow washing gently across my windshield, it suddenly occurred to me what that lesson might be.

"Maybe it's about love," I went on. "I mean, the outpouring of love I've received since Oliver was taken—maybe God or my parents in heaven are trying to open my eyes to all the love I never realized was there, you know?"

I kept going, believing I was on to something.

"I mean, the person who took Oliver . . . it was a terrible act. I hate the act . . . but I don't hate the person. In fact, I refuse to hate that person. Whoever it is, they just don't understand the love that is there between Oliver and me. He doesn't know how that love was created. He doesn't know what it means. And I can't judge him, because I don't know how he grew up. I don't know what compelled him to do this. Maybe he never learned to look at a dog as anything but a thing. Like he was stealing a cell phone or a purse and not this being that I love so much. He doesn't realize that what he stole from me was *my life*. Maybe this is just a misunderstanding. Whoever took Oliver just doesn't understand the power of that love."

I'd never voiced these ideas before. I'd never even had them, not even as vague thoughts. This all just poured out of me, and when it did, I felt physically and emotionally drained—but not in a bad way. It was like Isabela had relieved me of an enormous burden that had been crushing my chest simply by giving me the chance to talk.

"Steven, that is beautiful," Isabela finally said. "That is what you have to hold on to. *And that is what is going to bring Oliver back to you.* Hate can't do it. Only love will. So just hold on to that love."

Hold on to that love.

I was amazed. Who was this teenager expressing such a profound thought? How could she be so emotionally mature and so incredibly wise? And was she right?

Would love be the thing that brought Oliver back?

We arrived at the college after two hours on the road. I helped Isabela with her bags and told her to be careful not to slip in the snow. Before she left, she looked at me and smiled.

"Steven, you're going to get your dog back. Believe it."

"I will," I told her. "And thank you."

The snow was still falling in a steady but harmless way, and on my drive back home, I found that I felt better than I had in days. Something had changed. Unburdening my soul like that helped me focus on something other than my anger and resentment. Maybe this was about forgiveness. Maybe that's what I should focus on: forgiving whoever took Oliver.

Maybe that was the lesson I still needed to learn.

Focus on love. Approach the search for Oliver with love, and you'll be okay. Maybe God is showing you how to be a better human.

Maybe God is showing you how to be a better human.

Before I knew it, I was back in Bedford and parked in front of Bryce's home. I put the keys to the Jeep in the cup holder and walked across the driveway to my car. Before I could get in, I heard a sound that stopped me in my tracks.

A chime.

Twelve chimes in all. The Sutton Clock Tower bell was striking midnight.

I stood there in the falling snow and listened to the chimes. They were so pure, so beautiful, so comforting. I stood there and let the sounds wash over me, my breath frosting in the night air, my heart filling with every toll. What did this mean? What was happening? I didn't know for sure, but I got the feeling that these beautiful chimes served to connect this lovely small town. They turned a collection of homes and people into a real community.

We are a community, I thought. *That's what we humans do. We help each other. We support each other. We share love.*

I'd never really thought of myself as part of a community, because I didn't believe I really fit in anywhere. But maybe I was wrong. Maybe I was part of something bigger than me.

The last chime sounded. Its fading echo floated around me like the playful snow. I got in my car and drove down the road, heading home.

An Oliver Story

Oliver likes when I take him into the town of Bedford. We visit the library, then I take him across the street to the Bedford Green. It's a nice space for him to trot around on the grass while I read the paper on a bench. He likes when people say hello to him. We both have felt very accepted by the people of Bedford. It's been a nice community for the both of us.

Chapter 13

*A*round the same time I was picking up Isabela on the evening of February 18, a woman named Janice Connolly was settling in on her sofa to watch TV.

Janice was the kind of friendly, down-to-earth person you could sit and watch a ballgame with. Earlier that day she returned to her home in the town of Mount Vernon, twenty miles north of New York City, after a three-day-long dog-sitting job in someone else's house. For more than twenty years, Janice had been the office manager for a veterinary technician at a Yonkers animal clinic, and she also worked at an animal shelter. But the clinic closed three years ago, and now she worked part-time for a pet groomer. She was happy to be home, and after having dinner with her husband, Derek, she sat on her comfortable, teal-green sofa and turned on the evening news. Her two short-hair cats—tortoise-colored Ming and jet-black Ling—jumped up on the sofa with her.

She switched the channel to News 12 Westchester, her favorite news show that she watched every morning and every evening. Nothing on the night's newscast grabbed her attention until the reporter Lisa Reyes came on and showed a clip of a dog being chased around a driveway by a cat.

That's funny, she thought. *A cat chasing a dog.*

By the time her head hit her pillow that night, Janice had forgotten all about the funny little dog on TV.

Oliver's Thoughts

I am one of those dogs who watches TV. Whenever Stee goes to work, he always turns the TV on for me. I look for other dogs to bark at. It's really fun!

Call me crazy, but I think I saw my dad crying on the TV tonight. I had to play it cool, but I wanted to bark at the TV. Then I saw Willy chasing me! On TV! I just sat there and watched, but I swear it was Willy! Then I heard the people who were taking care of me say they had to get rid of me in the morning. Then they shut the TV off.

The next morning Janice got up at 6:30 a.m. and went to buy groceries at the food store on the corner. Janice lived in a four-story redbrick building on Norton Street, next to a vacant lot and a mechanic's shop. The block was in an area that had seen better days. But Janice liked living there because it was a real neighborhood—people looked out for each other. Like her husband, Derek, Janice was born and raised in nearby Yonkers, and Mount Vernon felt like home to her. And Norton Street had its own character, its own charm. It was a family block, a place full of friendly, caring people.

Janice walked out of the building and came down the five-step stoop. She noticed a big, white SUV parked in front of the building, and she recognized the young man behind the wheel. His name was Del, and he lived in the area. Some people liked to say bad things about Del, and it was true that he'd gotten into his share of trouble, but in Janice's mind, he was someone who hadn't received much guidance in his life and was trying to figure out where he fit into the world. She went over to the white SUV to say hello.

"What are you doing out so early, Del?" Janice asked.

"My mom won't let me in the house with the dog," he said.

Janice looked down and saw the dog. It was a little thing, curled up in a dog bed on the passenger seat. The dog looked up at Janice with big, timid eyes, and Janice thought, *Oh my goodness, he's so adorable.* She wondered where Del had gotten it, but she knew enough not to ask.

"Do you know anyone who wants a dog?" Del asked.

"I don't know, maybe," Janice said thoughtfully. "Let me take a picture."

Oliver's Thoughts

This lady is pointing one of those things at me, like Stee used to. Why? I guess I'll look at her. She seems nice. I wonder if she could help me find my dad. I know I saw him on TV last night.

Janice snapped a photo of the dog and asked Del for his phone number so she could call him in case she found a taker. Then she left to catch her Metro North train on her way to her job at the groomers. When she got to the store, Janice asked the groomer if she knew anyone who might want Del's little dog.

"I *do* know someone who is looking for a small dog," the groomer said.

Janice called Del to let him know.

"Okay," Del said. "I want $250 for the dog."

Janice was surprised, though she quickly realized she shouldn't have been. This was Del, after all. Always working an angle. She explained to him that no one would pay him for the dog—this was about finding the dog a good, safe home.

Del insisted on the payment.

"Okay, well, good luck then," Janice said, and she hung up.

A little while later a customer came into the grooming store with her dog. "He needs a bath," the customer said.

Janice took the little dog to the tiled basin, turned on the faucet, and tested the water to make sure it was warm. She was glad to see the dog didn't mind getting wet and in fact seemed to enjoy the process.

"Good boy," Janice told him as she lathered him up with shampoo. "Such a good boy."

The dog was a little black-and-brown Yorkie Terrier. Janice, who'd owned and loved many dogs and cats over the years, was impressed by the Yorkie's friendly demeanor. She knew some Yorkies could be snappy and high-strung, but not this one. This one was sweet and loving.

Come to think of it, Janice thought, *so was the dog in Del's white SUV.* That dog looked like a Yorkie too, and that dog had also seemed like a sweetheart. *How about that?* she thought. *Two sweet little Yorkies in one morning.*

Two sweet little Yorkies in one morning.

Then it hit her.

The dog in the white SUV—it had looked strangely familiar. She felt like she had seen him before . . . somewhere.

Of course! She had seen the dog on TV! The cute little dog being chased by a cat! The news report about a stolen dog in nearby Scarsdale! Was that the same dog in the SUV? Was that the dog everyone was looking for?

Or was it just a weird coincidence?

Janice pushed these thoughts out of her mind so she could focus on shampooing the Yorkie in the basin.

An Oliver Story

Oliver doesn't have many dog friends, but he is friends with Chico, the Terrier next door. Some mornings he'll go outside and sit in front of the sliding door to the house where Chico lives and just wait for him. When Chico finally comes out, Oliver says hello, and then they go off and play. It's pretty cool to have a friend like that.

The Search

Day Five
February 19

Chapter 14

On Monday night I decided not to stay at Laura's house and instead slept in an extra bedroom in Lucy's house in Bedford. It was my first time sleeping in a bed, not on a sofa, in five nights. I still couldn't bear to be in my own cottage without Oliver there, but at least I'd made it back to Lucy's place, which was *near* my cottage. That was progress.

When I woke up at 6:00 a.m., I still felt good from the night before—from my conversation with Isabela and from my midnight moment at the Sutton Clock Tower. At the same time, I still didn't have a single clue as to where Oliver was. I wasn't going to stop looking for him—not any time soon, maybe not ever. But even so, I had to prepare myself for never seeing him again. I had to accept that this was possible. And accepting that was the hardest thing I would ever have to do.

So before the old feelings of anger and resentment came

rushing back, I decided I wanted to somehow capture the wave of love and acceptance that had washed over me the night before.

I felt like I needed to make my thoughts known. And I knew that I wanted to do it on my own Facebook page.

I needed to make my thoughts known.

As I said, I wasn't much of a Facebook person. I rarely posted anything beyond a photo of Oliver or of my sisters and me. But now there was an entire post devoted to Oliver, and it was being followed by thousands of people.

Thousands! Nancy had handled all the updates so far, but I realized it was time for me to post something on my page too, to thank everyone for the outpouring of love.

It was time for me to share what was in my heart.

I asked Lucy if I could use the computer in her work room, and she said go right ahead. I sat at her desk and stared at the blank screen and wondered where to begin. The next hour was a blur, and when it was over I'd written a long essay I titled "I Am Caught in the Storm."

On one side of this storm, my life is destroyed. I can't sleep in my own bed. I can't go to the gym. I can't listen to music. I haven't listened to a song in four days. I can't go for my daily walk, because my companion is gone. I can't cook, because my buddy isn't there to eat with me. I can barely walk into my cottage to grab a change of clothes.

On the other side, I'm witnessing the support and love for me and my companion grow every day to monumental proportions. I'm either crying because I miss Oliver or crying because the love I'm feeling from everyone is incredible. I haven't had time to read all the comments, but from what I've read, I see the true spirit of humanity. I'm watching all this unfold before my eyes, and it's like witnessing a miracle.

I wrote about how my sisters would do anything to help me. I wrote about how I am a spiritual person who believes my mother and father and brother were looking out for me from heaven. I wrote about the patterns in my life and about the Carino way—one step forward, two steps back. And I spoke directly to Oliver.

I know you are frightened, and I know you miss me, as I do you. But I *know* that whoever has you right now loves you, because that is all any person could do when they are in your presence. It is *impossible* not to love you. My heart is breaking as I write this, but I know I will hold you again, because this person did not mean to destroy us. They just saw your beauty, and they took you for themselves. If you only knew how you are bringing out the very best in everyone, you would be amazed! Hold on, my little boy, and we will go for those walks again soon.

When I was done writing, I put my finger over the Return

key to post my essay. But I couldn't do it. I couldn't press the key. This was too personal, too honest, to share with the world. I sat in the chair for a long time, wondering if I should share the post or delete it.

Just then my cell phone sounded. "Hello?"

"Yes, hi, is this Steven?"

"Yes, this is Steven."

"Is your dog missing?"

"Yes, my dog is missing."

"Well, I'm calling about a dog I saw this morning that looks like your dog."

So far I'd received three or four calls from people who believed they'd spotted Oliver in some far-off place—a shelter in Iowa, a shelter in Florida, places like that. I'd asked them to send me photos, and none of the dogs were Oliver. So I wasn't terribly hopeful about this latest call.

"Okay, well, where did you see him?" I asked.

"In Mount Vernon. There's a guy down there, and he offered to sell me this dog for $250. And the dog was in a white SUV. I think the dog has been living in that SUV."

"How did you get my number?" I asked.

"I looked for it on Facebook after I saw the video with the dog and the cat."

"What video?"

"You know, the cat chasing the dog."

I wasn't aware that News 12 had run another report, this one featuring the video from my phone that Laura sent to the station.

That was news to me. But obviously, this person had seen it, and now she believed she'd seen Oliver.

"I think this guy who has him has been in and out of trouble," she continued. "I took the dog's picture in case I found someone who wanted the dog."

"You have a photo? Can you send it to me?"

The woman told me she would send me the photo as soon as she got to work.

"Where is the dog now?" I asked her. "Can you tell me where he is right now?"

"If he's still there, he's at 328 Norton Street in Mount Vernon."

The woman told me her name—Janice Connolly—and promised she would send me the photo. I hung up and realized my hands were shaking. *Wait for the photo*, I told myself. *Don't get all worked up, not yet. Wait for the photo.*

Wait for the photo.

Lucy came downstairs and asked me who I'd been talking to. I told her about Janice and the dog in the SUV.

"I'm waiting to see the photo," I said as calmly as I could.

"Well, maybe we should go there now, just in case," Lucy said. "Are you doing anything else?"

In fact, I wasn't doing anything at all. I hadn't made plans for that day. There was no reason I couldn't drive to Mount Vernon, a town about thirty minutes away, on the outside chance the dog in the SUV was Oliver.

I'm coming with you.

"Okay," I told Lucy, "I'll do it. I'll go there now."

"I'm coming with you," Lucy said.

"Okay, fine. Just let me do one thing before we go."

I went back to Lucy's computer and looked over what I'd written one last time. Then I hit the Return key to post my little statement to the Facebook page and went upstairs to get ready to go to Mount Vernon.

Chapter 15

I was on my way to Mount Vernon when I got a text alert on my cell phone. I opened the text, and I saw it was from Janice. It was a photo. I was almost too nervous to look at it. What if it wasn't Oliver? Had I gotten my hopes up despite trying so hard not to? How would I react if it wasn't him?

I took a deep breath and looked at the photo of the dog, who was curled up in a square bed in the passenger seat of an SUV. Then I nearly drove off the Hutchinson River Parkway.

"It's him!" I screamed.

"What?" Lucy said.

"The picture. It's him! It's Oliver!"

I handed the phone to Lucy and asked, "Is it him?"

"It looks like him."

"I know, but is it him?"

"Oh my goodness, it *is* him."

"It is him, right? It's Oliver. But is it really him?"

"Steven, it's him. Look at him. That's Oliver!"

"I know, that's Oliver. That dog is Oliver! But is it really him?"

I didn't know how to react. Cautiously? Joyously? I knew it was Oliver in the photo. I knew it the instant I saw it. The way he was curled up, the way he looked up at Janice, his ears, his little nose—that was Oliver! And he was acting just like I knew he would—he was playing it cool! Part of me, though, could hardly believe it was him. Was it possible that I could be on the verge of getting Oliver back? Would that kind of miracle ever really happen to me?

> Was it possible that I could be on the verge of getting Oliver back?

"I'm calling the Mount Vernon police," I told Lucy. "We need them there when we approach this guy."

I got through to the police station and told the desk sergeant about Oliver. I told him exactly where Oliver was and how they had to hurry up and get him before this guy in the SUV took off.

"Okay, we'll send someone out," the sergeant said.

Then I called Laura and told her we were five minutes from her house.

"Be ready to jump in the car," I said. "It's Oliver! It's him in the photo! He's in Mount Vernon!"

Oliver's Thoughts

Why is this man taking me out of the car and bringing me back upstairs? I just want to stay in the car. I thought we were going to see Stee. I'm so confused. Where is my dad?

Laura was waiting in her driveway when we pulled up. She got in, and I drove down the Bronx River Parkway as fast as I could, careful not to speed too much. It took us twenty minutes to arrive in Mount Vernon. The GPS steered us toward Norton Street.

When I turned the corner onto the street, I almost couldn't breathe. It was all too much. The possibility that Oliver was there. The possibility that he wasn't. I gripped the steering wheel and slowly worked my way down the block, looking for the mysterious white SUV.

Then I saw it. It was right where Janice had said it was—in the middle of the block, outside 328 Norton Street. I pulled the car to the curb and jumped out and ran toward the SUV. There was no one in the driver's seat, but I didn't care—all I cared about was Oliver. I got to the car and ran around to the passenger side and looked through the window.

"Oliver!" I yelled out. But he wasn't there. The seat was empty.

I looked through all the windows, and Oliver wasn't anywhere.

All I cared about was Oliver.

Just then I noticed the two young uniformed police officers standing behind the white SUV.

Laura came up behind me. She saw my expression and turned to the cops.

"Where's the dog?" she asked.

"What dog?" one of the officers said.

"My brother's dog. He was in the car. Somebody took him, and he was in this car."

"We didn't see any dog here, lady."

"What are you talking about?" I said. "He was here! He was right here just a while ago!"

"We don't know about any dog," the cop said. "All we know is we ran these plates and this car is stolen. But we never saw a dog."

Here it was again—the Carino Curse. The SUV was there, but Oliver wasn't. *Of course* he wasn't. I'd warned myself not to get my hopes up, and yet I had. I fully expected to see Oliver sitting in that passenger seat. What was I thinking?

Why would I have ignored my own history? Didn't I know the Carino Curse was patient and persistent? That it would give me a little, then always snatch it away?

"Look, we'll keep an eye out for your dog," one of the officers said. "But be careful out here. Watch your back."

I took one last look into the SUV, just to be sure. It was empty, just like it had been before. Oliver wasn't there. Oliver was gone again.

But maybe, just maybe, Oliver wasn't too far away.

Chapter 16

*I*n the fourth grade I kept my hair slicked down, wore gigantic gold wire-framed glasses, and carried my schoolbooks in a brown fake-leather briefcase. I didn't realize all three of those things made me the biggest nerd in class. Most of the kids carried their books in their arms, but I loved my briefcase—it made me feel very official. So I walked around with it for the whole year.

One day during class, our teacher, Mr. Adams, was talking with students gathered around his desk. I walked by and overheard what they were talking about—US presidents.

Naturally, I sidled over.

"Was there ever a president who was elected and then lost, then got elected again?" one of the students asked.

"Yes, I think so," Mr. Adams said. "I can't think of his name offhand."

"Grover Cleveland," I announced.

The students turned to look at me standing there, somewhat smugly, with my big glasses and my briefcase.

"How do you know that?" one student asked.

"I just do," I said. "Grover Cleveland, the twenty-second and twenty-fourth president. In between was Benjamin Harrison."

Mr. Adams pulled out an encyclopedia and checked. Then he looked at me quizzically. He asked me what else I knew about Grover Cleveland. I said he was born in 1837 and died in 1908, and he served from 1885 to 1889 and again from 1893 to 1897. And he was a Democrat. Mr. Adams asked if I knew anything about any other presidents. I rattled off some facts about Andrew Jackson. He asked if I had a favorite president.

"Harry S. Truman," I said. "He's eighty-eight years old now, and I'm rooting for him to make it past the oldest ex-president, John Adams, who was ninety."

"How do you know all this?" Mr. Adams asked.

As proudly as I could, I said, "My mother taught me."

Mr. Adams looked at me with amazement. He was a big man with a crew cut, and he'd been wounded in World War II. Sometimes he walked with crutches; sometimes he used a wheelchair. Mr. Adams *loved* American history, and he challenged his students to memorize the Gettysburg Address. Every morning, he led us in saluting the flag. Not surprisingly, he got a big kick out of me knowing all the presidents, and eventually, like my father, he would walk down the hallway with me, stop other teachers, and tell them to "pick a number" between one and thirty-seven.

I never let him down. This, of course, did not help my reputation as a nerd.

"You know," Mr. Adams told me that day, "you can write a letter to President Truman, and we can mail it to him."

I was astonished. I didn't know an ordinary person could write to a US president. Mr. Adams assured me that he would get the address, and Mr. Truman would receive the letter. That night, I sat down with my mother, and together we composed a short little note in which I told Mr. Truman that I knew the names of all the presidents, that he was my favorite president, and I hoped that one day I could be president too.

Less than one month later, my mother picked me up from my organ lesson with a funny little smile on her face.

"You have something special waiting at home," she said.

"What is it?"

"Oh, I don't know. A letter from President Truman."

My eyes nearly popped out of my head. We drove home, me urging my mom to go faster, and when we got there, I raced inside and snatched the letter off the kitchen table. I marveled at the elegant off-white envelope, which had Mr. Truman's big, bold signature across the date stamp, just above my name—*my name!*—Steven Carino.

When I opened it, I saw the letter wasn't actually written by President Truman; it was from his personal secretary, Rose A. Conway. But that hardly mattered. I figured Mr. Truman was a busy man. In fact, he was very sick at the time and would pass away just two months later. For me, it was more than enough to know he had read my letter and was encouraging me to keep up with my interest in US presidents. "History was his favorite subject," Ms. Conway explained to me in the letter, "and proved an invaluable help to him in his public life."

And finally: "Mr. Truman sends you his personal best wishes for a long, happy, and useful life."

I was blown away. My mother had the letter framed, and we hung it up on my bedroom wall. It was one of the best moments of my childhood and also one of my favorite memories of my mother. I could see on her face how very proud she was of me. It was a look I will never, ever forget.

It wasn't lost on me that my search for Oliver had led me to a place called Mount Vernon—named for the Virginia plantation of George Washington. The area was the scene of several Revolutionary War battles, inspiring new settlers there in the 1850s to give it a presidential name. Now the boy who knew all the presidents was there, trying to find his dog.

Mount Vernon is not a small town. With nearly seventy thousand residents, it's the eighth most populous city in New York State. It's also one of the most ethnically diverse cities in the county. Whites, Blacks, Latinos, Asians, Native Americans, Brazilians, and others share its streets. Part of the city boasts million-dollar homes. Other parts are mainly apartments and split-family dwellings. There is a little bit of everything in Mount Vernon; it's a hard city to characterize in any uniform way.

All that mattered about Mount Vernon to us, though, was that Oliver was somewhere in it.

While we were talking to the police officers, my cell phone rang. My friend Tony Marcogliese was calling. He is a colorful character who works in the garbage business, and I'd known him for about eight years. We met through a mutual friend and got along pretty well. When Tony tore up his foot and landed in the hospital, I went to see him a couple of times to cheer him up—something he was hugely grateful for and never forgot. When I was down on my luck and scraping out a living by driving a limo, Tony would hire me to take him into New York City and hand me a hundred-dollar bill, at least double the fare. We didn't talk or get together all that often, but we had the kind of friendship where we knew we'd be there for each other in difficult times.

We knew we'd be there for each other in difficult times.

And this was a difficult time.

"Steven, I heard about Oliver," Tony said. "I'm so sorry, man. How are you holding up?"

"Tony, I'm in Mount Vernon looking for him! Someone just spotted him a while ago!"

"Wait, what? Where are you? I'm coming down."

"Tony, you don't have to do that."

"Give me the address, and I'll be right there."

I didn't argue. Tony lived thirty miles away in Pound Ridge. I knew he would come even if I insisted otherwise.

Laura, Lucy, and I stood on Norton Street and watched a police tow truck take away the white SUV. After five days of having no idea where Oliver was, it was breathtaking to know where he'd physically been just a little bit earlier. My Oliver had sat in that very car just hours ago! It was almost as if I could still feel him there, which was why it was so hard to watch the police take the SUV. On the plus side, we'd narrowed our search area from the entire world to, hopefully, a square mile or so in Mount Vernon. Still, a square mile gives you a whole bunch of places to hide a twelve-pound dog.

> We'd narrowed our search area from the entire world to, hopefully, a square mile.

"Okay, so what are we going to do?" Lucy asked.

"We have to ask around about Oliver," Laura said. "Someone must have seen him. Let's start over there."

Laura walked to the mechanic shop next to a fenced-in lot. Two men in gray mechanic's outfits were standing outside the shop. One was older and had white whiskers. The other was younger and stocky. We went over and showed them Oliver's photo. I guess I expected them not to be very welcoming to us, but in fact they were immediately friendly and helpful.

"This kid poked his head in this morning and said he had a cute dog for sale for $250," Terry, the older mechanic, said. "I asked him where the dog was, and he said in the car."

"So you never saw the dog?" I asked.

"No, because we told him we weren't interested," Terry said. "It's funny—my wife and I saw the TV report about a stolen dog last night. You know, with the cat chasing the dog? We were watching it and laughing our heads off. But I didn't realize that was the same dog the kid was selling."

Like Janice, Terry had made the connection too late. "Do you know who this kid is?" I asked.

The two men were suddenly quiet. They looked at each other but didn't say a word. Finally, Rolando, the younger of the two mechanics, said, "Yeah, I know him. He wears a baseball cap. He's known to be a bit of a troublemaker."

"Do you happen to know where he lives?"

Rolando hesitated again. Then he pointed at the four-story redbrick building down the street, right where the white SUV had been parked.

"He lives in that building," Rolando said.

Oliver's Thoughts

Why is this man leaving me at the back of this building, outside and alone? But it's not a time for me to be scared. I've got to be brave. Maybe this is my chance to find my dad. I'm getting outta here.

Terry and Rolando let us put up flyers outside their shop and promised they'd keep an eye out for the kid and for Oliver. Laura, Lucy, and I regrouped. Now that we knew where the person who took Oliver lived, what were we going to do?

Wait for him to come back? Go in and ask around about him? Call the cops again? It was Laura who came up with a plan.

"Lucy and I will go back to my house and print up more flyers," she said. "We need to *plaster* the area with flyers. Also, give me that lady's phone number. I want to talk to her."

I gave her Janice Connolly's number. If anyone could get more information out of her, it was Laura.

"When Tony gets here, you two can ask around and see what else you can find out," Laura said.

Tony showed up just a few minutes later.

Tony isn't the type of guy to make a quiet entrance. He is, to say the least, distinctive. I watched him steer his big black Range Rover down Norton Street and park it across from the redbrick building. I watched as the door opened and Tony stepped out. He was wearing a multicolor fur coat and thick black sunglasses. His dark, graying hair was slicked back like a gangster. He had on a T-shirt, jeans, and huge boots. If you didn't know him, you might think he was trouble. In fact, he was one of the sweetest, most generous men I'd ever known.

"Steven," he said, before wrapping me in a big bear hug.

"You didn't have to come down," I said. "I've got people helping me find Oliver."

"Steven, I know how much you love your dog, but I didn't come down here for Oliver," Tony said. "I came down here for you. You're my friend, and I'd do anything for you."

You're my friend, and I'd do anything for you.

I don't think Tony had any idea how much those words meant to me at that precise moment.

"So let's get to it," Tony said. "Let's find Oliver."

We got in Tony's Range Rover and drove around the block, looking for the kid in a baseball cap. We stopped at a deli at the corner of Norton Street, and I asked the woman behind the counter if she'd seen anyone selling a dog.

"Yes, he was in here this morning," she said. "He was trying to sell me this dog he had in the car."

We got back in the Range Rover and drove back down Norton Street. Rolando, the mechanic, flagged me down.

"Follow me," he said. "I think I may know where your dog is."

My heart pounded in my chest like a drum.

Rolando took us to the vacant lot next to the redbrick building where the kid in the baseball cap lived.

"There's a lady back here who thinks she heard a dog barking," Rolando said.

We went to a little courtyard behind the building. I was running, not walking. A woman in her forties was there. She had two children, neither older than ten, with her. They appeared to be fanning out and looking for Oliver.

"My kids heard a little dog barking in the back of the building," she explained to me. "So I came out back, but he's not here."

I looked into the courtyard. It was a small, grim place.

It might have been a really nice courtyard at one point, but now it looked more like a garbage dump surrounded by a six-foot-tall chain link fence. The fence was partly torn down and shredded in spots. Only small patches of grass remained, and those were covered with junk—a mattress, old clothes, cans and bottles. I pulled apart the torn fencing and squeezed into the yard, searching every last inch for Oliver. But by then it was obvious Oliver wasn't there.

"Maybe he's still around here somewhere," Tony said.

"What's his name?" the mother asked.

"Oliver."

She told her young children to walk around and call out Oliver's name. Tony and I called out his name too. We searched the entire vacant lot to the right of the redbrick building, until we wound up on the avenue behind Norton Street. I looked at the street sign and was struck by the name: Garfield Avenue. Like James A. Garfield. Another president.

What is it with all the president stuff? I wondered.

To our right, we saw a sprawling, fenced-in lot filled with construction equipment, traffic cones, and a big red dump truck. My first thought was, *There are a lot of places for a dog to hide in there.* If whoever took Oliver had put him in the courtyard, and if Oliver had snuck out and walked away, he'd probably look for a secluded place to lie down. Oliver could be in this lot.

I tried to open the fence door, but it was securely fastened with a thick chain and padlock. The top of the fence was ringed with barbed wire. There was no way in.

"Look there," I said to Tony, pointing to a small gap of about a foot between the bottom of the fence and the concrete pavement. "If we try to lift that a little, I can get in."

Tony squatted and pulled at the bottom of the fence with all his might. It gave another few inches. I got down on my stomach and began to slither under. I was possessed, crawling through the dirt with abandon to somehow get to Oliver. I got stuck several times, but I kept squirming through, my pants and shirt ripping against the concrete, my fingers clawing at the ground to pull me forward. Tony summoned all his strength and gave the fence a mighty tug, and with a final surge I was through. I stood up covered in dust and dirt.

Rolando, the mechanic, had watched the whole thing. "That is one crazy dude," he said to Tony.

"You don't know how much this dog means to him," Tony replied.

I ran through the lot, calling Oliver's name, crawling under trucks, pulling at heavy wood pallets, frantically searching every little corner. It took me close to an hour to check the entire lot. By the end of it, I was sweating, breathing heavily, and black with filth and grime.

And *still*—I didn't find Oliver.

An Oliver Story

Oliver doesn't like loud noises. He doesn't like disruptions of any kind. Even when I make my bed, all the fluffing of sheets and tossing of pillows is too much for him, and he runs and hides under the dresser—which is okay with me, because I don't like loud noises either.

Chapter 17

It all began way, way back with a dog named Michael.

Michael was a medium-sized Yorkshire Terrier my sister Nancy brought home when I was nine. I didn't pay all that much attention to Michael, because back then my mother was still alive and I got all the love and attention I needed from her. But less than two years after Michael arrived, my mother was diagnosed with cancer.

During my mother's illness, the mood in our house became pretty grim. I have no doubt that all the sadness in our lives affected our pets too. After all, dogs are hugely sensitive to people's moods.

In the middle of it all, my father got laid off from his job. It was a hard year for our family. Soon after that, Michael got hit by a car. My father rushed him to the hospital, but Michael didn't make it.

Before he passed, Michael had fathered six puppies that were staying with our aunt. Being the youngest, I was allowed to pick one for us to bring home. I chose the last one to be born, and I named her Marcie. As my mother got sicker, Marcie and I grew closer.

After my mother passed away, Marcie and I became inseparable. She was always there for me whenever I needed her.

> The thing that kept me going was Marcie's unconditional love.

And, boy, did I need her a lot. Marcie got me through the unhappy years of my childhood and the miserable parts of my teenage years. You see, as a teenager, I was a mess. I was chubby, pimple-faced, and always worried about something. After being the smart young boy who did everything right, I was suddenly the weirdo who did everything wrong. There were days when I felt so confused and so very sad. The thing that kept me going was Marcie's unconditional love.

When I turned eighteen, I had to leave for college—and leave Marcie behind. It was one of the hardest things I've ever had to do. Marcie was never just a dog or a pet to me.

She was, in many ways, the emotional center of my complicated life. In my sophomore year in college, my father called to tell me Marcie had died. I felt guilty for not being there when she needed me, and even today I still do.

From then on, dogs became the one constant thing I could count on in my crazy, mixed-up life. After college I lived in a little studio apartment in New York City and worked for an advertising agency. But I still had no confidence and was generally unhappy. Someone suggested I get a puppy, hoping it might make me feel better. So I did.

She was an uncommonly adorable apricot-colored poodle, and I named her Coffee. Coffee changed my life. She gave me a sense of purpose and identity that had not been there before. When I walked her around my neighborhood, I couldn't go a block without someone stopping me to play with her and tell me how cute she was. One time a police car pulled up next to me, and the cop who was driving called out to me. I wondered what I did wrong.

"Excuse me," the cop said, "do you mind if we say hello to your dog?"

Coffee became the one thing my whole life could revolve around. Everything else was less important and would eventually fall into place. She filled my dingy little apartment with playfulness and joy, and she filled my life with meaning and hope. I had felt empty ever since the day my mother passed away. I never imagined that a tiny eight-pound dog could ever fill that hole, but that's just what Coffee did.

She filled my life with meaning and hope.

And so it went for pretty much my whole life. When I started a computer consulting business and began earning a lot of money,

Coffee was there to make me feel unstoppable. And when the business went bust and I was out of a job, Coffee was there to remind me not to get too down about it. It was just around then that I decided Coffee deserved a little friend of her own to play with, and I got another dog, another apricot poodle I named Mickey, after one of my favorite baseball players, Mickey Mantle. At first Coffee wasn't crazy about having a brother, but Mickey was so friendly she eventually came around. As for Mickey and me, well, we became really great friends. Like Coffee, he became my little buddy—as much a part of me as my arm or my heart.

Over the years more wonderful dogs came into my life.

There was a beautiful Yorkie–Shih Tzu mix named Louie, who was a complete character with a huge personality. I almost can't explain how special our bond was. It was Louie and Mickey who together got me through one of the hardest times of my life. It was pretty much my rock bottom—no career, no relationship, and practically no money. Louie and Mickey kept me going. We needed a new place to live, so I looked through the classified ads in a newspaper for rental apartments and found Lucy's cottage, where I still live.

There is almost nothing bad about owning a dog.

There is almost nothing bad about owning a dog. They improve our lives and bring us so much happiness. But one bad thing is that they don't live as long as we'd like them to. I eventually lost Coffee, Louie and Mickey to the passage of time. Without them, I was completely gutted. And then another angel came forward and saved my life.

Oliver.

Oliver and I became inseparable, bound to each other in ways neither of us fully understood. All we knew for sure was that as long as we were together, nothing could really hurt us. Together, we would always—*always*—be okay.

And then, on Valentine's Day, Oliver was stolen, and suddenly we weren't together anymore.

An Oliver Story

Oliver doesn't like it when I pay attention to other dogs. So if I reach down to pet Chico, the dog that lives next door, Oliver starts barking. Not in a mean way, just in a way that says, "Hey! What about me?" Even if I pet Anna Belle, the miniature cow, Oliver barks at me. I have to keep assuring him, "Don't worry, Oliver. You know you're my favorite puppy ever." I guess we all need to hear that kind of thing once in a while.

Chapter 18

*B*ack in Mount Vernon, Tony helped me crawl under the fence and get out of the lot. My heart was still pounding, and my body was shaking. I hadn't found Oliver, but I had the strange feeling that he was somewhere nearby. And I was afraid if I stopped looking, even for a minute, I would lose his trail.

Or maybe I was just fooling myself.

We decided to walk around the area and see who else might know the kid in the baseball cap. We spoke with five or six people. Some of them knew the kid, some didn't, but none had any information about Oliver. Still, every single one of them was friendly and concerned. I'm not sure what I'd been expecting, but the openness of the people in the neighborhood surprised me. Their sincere interest gave me the impression that they lived under a code where if one person in the community had a problem, they *all* had a problem. It didn't even matter if you were a stranger to them; if they could help you, they would, no questions asked.

"You know something?" Tony said as we walked around the area. "The people here are genuinely concerned about you and Oliver. They're such nice people."

"I was just thinking the same thing."

Here was something else that, just maybe, God was trying to open my eyes to. Yet another lesson I still needed to learn.

Maybe there was more to the story.

The assumptions I'd made about the neighborhood from just driving through it were, I now realized, simplistic and wrong. Yes, the person who took Oliver did something terrible. But what did I know about this person? Maybe there was more to the story than I could imagine. I thought about what Isabela had told me on our drive up to Bard College—it would be love and compassion, not hate and judgment, that would bring Oliver home. Was that what was happening now?

My cell phone sounded. It was Laura. She had talked with Janice Connolly and had gone to see her at the pet-grooming store where she worked. Janice gave her a new lead.

"Steven, go into that building and go up to apartment 3S," Laura said.

"What's in 3S?"

"It's Janice's apartment. Her husband is there now. She says he knows where Oliver is."

"What?"

"You have to go talk to him. And bring Tony with you."

Tony and I walked into the redbrick building through an unlocked glass front door. We walked up the stairs to the third floor. The hallway was dark and quiet. We approached 3S and stopped in front of it. We looked at each other, and I took a deep breath and knocked.

The door opened to reveal three big, burly men. All of them were well over six feet tall. One of them, the one who was sitting in a chair, motioned to us.

"Come on in, fellas," he said.

He introduced himself as Derek, Janice's husband. "My wife told me you're missing a dog."

"Yes. Oliver," I said. "He was stolen."

"Okay, listen. The dog was in apartment 2W. The kid who lives there is always in and out of trouble. I know the dog was in that apartment because I heard him barking."

Now we knew exactly where the kid in the baseball cap lived. The logical next step was to visit his apartment and look for Oliver. But Derek told us to check the roof first.

"He might have seen the cops when they came for the car," Derek said. "Maybe he stashed the dog on the roof. Sometimes people hide stuff up there."

I thanked Derek for seeing us and for the information.

"Good luck finding your dog," he said. His two burly friends wished us good luck too.

We walked up another flight and found the door to the roof. It wasn't locked, but it was stuck, and we couldn't open it.

Tony turned sideways and rammed the door with his right shoulder, like a running back plowing through a tackle. He gave the door a pretty good hit, then another. In his fur coat and dark sunglasses, he looked like an undercover cop making an arrest. As Tony kept bashing the door, I felt a smile come over my face. It wasn't my doing; it just happened. I hadn't smiled in so long, it felt strange.

Tony looked at me and said, "What's so funny?"

"Look at us," I said. "This is like a movie. A guy in a fur coat trying to knock down a door. How is this my life?"

Tony smiled too, then went back to the door. Finally, he managed to push it open. We went up on the roof and looked around, the layers and layers of black tar slightly squishy beneath our feet. It didn't take long to see that Oliver wasn't there. Tony and I stood by the roof wall and looked down over the neighborhood. We could see for blocks and blocks in any direction. Being so high above the streets felt special and peaceful. It was like, after digging down into the nitty-gritty of Oliver's theft, we were suddenly being given a broader overview. A new perspective. Both Tony and I were quiet for a while, looking out over the town.

Down on the street, five stories below, I recognized Rolando, the mechanic, looking up at me and shaking his head, as if to say, "This guy really *is* crazy."

Suddenly, it was Tony who started laughing. I laughed along with him. Neither of us felt the need to explain why we were giggling like two school kids.

"This is the first time I've laughed all week," I said.

Tony looked at me and put his hand on my shoulder. "We're gonna get him back. You know that, right?"

I didn't reply, because I didn't know if I believed him. "So what do you want to do now?" Tony asked.

"I guess we go to apartment 2W."

We walked down to the second floor, and Tony stood behind me as I got ready to knock on the door of the apartment. What if Oliver was there? What if he wasn't? I had no idea what I would do in either case. Finally, I rapped on the door three times with my knuckles.

We're gonna get him back.

After a few seconds, the door opened just a crack. I could see one eye looking at me through the small opening. Then the door opened wider, and I saw a woman in her early forties standing there.

The same woman who had helped us search for Oliver in the courtyard.

"You?" I said.

"Yeah, it's me," she said.

"But you helped me look for him," I said. "How could Oliver be here if you helped me look for him?"

"He's not here," she said. "Why would I help you look for him if I already had him?"

"But someone told me they heard my dog in here."

"There's no dog here," she said.

I was confused. Derek had been certain he heard a dog in 2W. And he knew the kid in the baseball cap lived there.

"Well, maybe it's your son who has him," I said.

The woman's expression quickly changed. "Everyone in this building blames my son for everything, and I'm sick and tired of it," she said. "You don't know this area. You don't live here. You don't know my son. So, no, I don't have your dog."

With that, she closed and locked the door.

My first thought was that Oliver wasn't in her apartment. If he'd been there, he would have heard my voice and barked. He would have let me know he was there. Even so, the only way I could know for sure was to look through the apartment myself. But I didn't want to knock on the door again and get in a screaming match. Instead, Tony and I went down to the street to figure out our next move.

Laura and Lucy were outside the building. They had just returned from White Plains with more flyers. I filled them in on what happened. Laura believed the first thing we should do was fan out and put up flyers. Every window, every pole, every corner. That way we could spread the word about the $5,000 reward and give people more incentive to come forward. We each took a small stack of flyers and began taping them up.

After I put up a single flyer, though, I had to stop.

I hadn't had flyer duty yet, so I'd never had to look too hard at the flyer itself. When I finally did, the big, bright picture of Oliver was too much for me to bear. It had been days since I'd had a close look at Oliver's innocent face, and suddenly seeing him on the flyer hit me harder than I expected. I felt my knees weaken again, followed by a sudden surge of anger.

"I can't do this," I told Tony. "I have to go back to apartment 2W."

I was in the redbrick building again, marching up to the second floor. I was by myself this time; I felt it should be just me, talking to the woman one on one. I knocked on the door and heard the shuffling of feet. When the door opened, this time it was a man standing there. The woman was standing behind him.

"Look," I said, "all I want is my dog. I need my dog. Where is my dog?"

"We don't have your dog," the man said calmly.

"A guy in the building told me he was here. Maybe he's not here now, but he *was* here—that I know. All I want is to get him back and take him home. That's all. I don't care about anything else. I just need my dog."

The woman stepped forward and opened the door wider. "You can come in and look for him if you like," she said. "But we don't have him."

"There's a $5,000 reward," I said. "I will give you the money right now. Just please, please tell me where he is."

I was starting to get emotional, and the man and woman looked at me like they felt sorry for me. They weren't mean or angry. Heck, they didn't even have to open the door for me, much less invite me into their home. Yet they patiently listened to me and seemed to genuinely feel bad for me. Standing there, I realized I believed them. I didn't have to search their apartment; Oliver wasn't there.

I believed them.

And, obviously, if their son was the person who took Oliver, they would be protective of him. I understood that too. My hope was that they would at least have an idea where Oliver might be, but they insisted that they didn't.

"We know how much you love that dog," the man said. "We just don't know where he is."

I thanked the couple in 2W and asked them to let me know if they heard anything about Oliver. They promised they would and closed the door. I walked downstairs and out onto the street.

"So what do you want to do now?" Laura asked.

"I don't know," I said. "All I know is I don't want to leave Mount Vernon yet."

We all got into Tony's Range Rover and talked strategy. It was late afternoon by then, and soon it would be dark. A few minutes later a car pulled up alongside us. It was Alan. He'd come to pick up Lucy and drive her home. I hugged Lucy and thanked her and told her how much it meant to me that she spent the day with me searching for Oliver.

"We will find him, Steven," Lucy assured me.

After Lucy and Alan left, Laura, Tony, and I sat in the warm Range Rover and reflected on our strange day. We talked about how friendly and helpful everyone was, even the couple in apartment 2W. We told Laura the story of our adventure on the roof. The day had been so filled with twists and turns that I never stopped to think that I hadn't eaten a thing. We'd all been on the go since Janice Connolly's phone call. Taking a break to eat something hadn't occurred to any of us.

And just then—*just then*—a car pulled up alongside us.

It was Alan again. I wondered why he'd come back, and I hoped nothing was wrong. Lucy got out of the car holding a big flat white box.

"We brought pizza!" she said cheerily.

Lucy hadn't just brought pizza. She'd brought a cheese pie from the legendary, family-owned Johnny's Pizzeria. I'd heard about the place, and it was famous for its tasty pizza. It had been in Mount Vernon for seventy-five years, and it only sold pizza by the pie, not the slice. When the sweet smell of cheese and sauce filled the Range Rover, I felt something that resembled genuine excitement. We each took a slice and bit into what was, for me, the single most delicious thing I'd ever tasted—ever. I don't know if it was the circumstances or the pizza, but to this day that slice remains my most memorable meal.

I looked around at Lucy and Alan and Laura and Tony

and told myself to take note of the moment. *These people, these wonderful people—they are here for you, Steven,* I thought. *Think of their thoughtfulness, one human to another—what a beautiful thing that is. Aren't you just blown away by them? By all of them? By the mechanics and the little kids who went around yelling Oliver's name, and by Janice and Derek and all the people on the street who stopped to talk to you? By your sister Laura and your pal Tony? By Alan and Lucy bringing pizza? How could you ever think you were all alone, Steven? Can't you tell you're not alone?*

Before we decided to call it a day, I spotted Rolando and Terry outside their store and went over to talk to them. "Guys, I didn't find Oliver," I told them, "but you know what? I am so touched by how everyone helped me. The people here are amazing."

"Well, you're not accusing anyone," Rolando said. "You're not screaming at anyone. You're being nice. It works both ways."

It pained me to leave Mount Vernon and drive back to Laura's house without Oliver. I tried not to think of where he might be or what had happened to him after he was spotted in the SUV. Had the kid in the baseball cap seen the police officers towing the stolen SUV and gotten scared? Had he stashed Oliver in the courtyard in case the cops came looking for him? And had Oliver made his way through the broken fence and run off? Or had the kid already sold Oliver to another stranger? I forced myself to stop going over the possibilities. There was no point to it. I just had to hold on to the slight bit of hope I had and keep searching.

Back at Laura's, I learned that my post on Facebook from earlier that day, the one titled "I Am Caught in the Storm," had received dozens and dozens of comments. Some people said the post made them cry. Others who read an update Nancy posted said they were going to go to Mount Vernon with $250 of their own money to try to buy Oliver. Some asked if they could share my post with their prayer groups. Nearly everyone offered their love and prayers and thanked me for baring my soul.

Plus, we were over ten thousand shares and likes.

Something was happening. Something that was bigger than me. My eyes were being opened to a greater truth about the world, a close-up look at the extraordinary power of love and empathy. Though I still hadn't found my beloved Oliver, that day in Mount Vernon, New York, was unquestionably one of the most beautiful days of my life.

An Oliver Story

Oliver likes it when I play my favorite songs on my record player. I'll say, "Hey, Oliver, want to listen to some Elvis or Sam Cooke this morning?" and Oliver will settle in on the bed or the chair to listen. He doesn't even mind if I start to sing along. One day I played the song "Take the Long Way Home" by Supertramp, and suddenly Oliver started to howl. I mean, he arched his neck and howled at the moon like a furry little wolf! Did that mean he loved the song or hated it? I guess I'll never know.

The Search

Day Six
February 20

Chapter 19

The day after Oliver disappeared, I took everything that reminded me of him and put it away in a closet. I took all of his toys and his towel out of my SUV. I picked up his red doggie bowl and his little mat with a map on it. And I grabbed his blue dog blanket, his dog bones, and his rubber fire hydrant chew toy—and I put them all where I wouldn't have to see them. I told myself that all of this was only temporary and that when Oliver came back, I'd bring out all his things and buy him a ton of new stuff too.

But as time passed, I couldn't stop imagining the day when I'd have to throw Oliver's things away.

When I woke up Wednesday morning in Laura's house, that was the terrible thought that came to me: *What if you never find Oliver? What will you do without Oliver? What will your life be like then?* Quickly, I got a grip on myself and forced myself to be positive. I hadn't lost Oliver yet. He was still out there, waiting for me to find him. All I had to do was not give up and keep going. Keep being positive.

Love and forgiveness, not anger and hate.

Love and forgiveness, not anger and hate. Oliver is depending on you.

I thought about something that happened before Oliver got stolen. When I was a kid going to school, I used to read the Bible with my parents, but as I got older, I didn't really read the Bible anymore. One day, for some reason, a line of Scripture popped into my mind.

It was from Proverbs 3:3: "Let love and faithfulness never leave you; bind them around your neck, write them on the tablet of your heart." I had always thought that was one of the most beautiful lines I'd ever read, and it felt good to have it in my mind again.

Then I decided I wanted to try to memorize all thirty-five verses of Proverbs 3. I'd always prided myself on my memorization skills, starting, of course, with the US presidents. But I hadn't tried to memorize anything for more than forty years—since my mother died. Now here was something else besides the presidents that mattered to me.

Why not commit it to memory? If nothing else, it would be a way to keep my mind sharp.

So when Oliver and I went on our daily walks around Lucy's farm, I would recite Proverbs 3 to him, and he would look back at me and listen to the words, as if he understood what they meant. Who knows, maybe he did. Our friendship really blossomed during those wonderful walks, and another line from Proverbs 3 suddenly had new meaning for me: "Blessed are those who find wisdom, those who gain understanding, for she is more profitable than silver and yields better returns than gold" (vv. 13–14).

Wow, I thought. *Could it really be true that wisdom and understanding are more valuable than silver and gold?* During those walks with Oliver, I began to realize what these words really meant. You see, it isn't so much what a person *has* that defines who they are;

Could it really be true that wisdom and understanding are more valuable than silver and gold?

it's what a person *believes*. Okay, so maybe I didn't have a lot of money, and I lived in a one-room cottage, and maybe in some people's minds that meant I was poor. But in *my* mind, I lived on a beautiful farm, I had three great sisters who loved me, and I had Oliver. That made me a *wealthy* man. How could I believe my life was cursed if I had Oliver by my side? Having Oliver made me *blessed*! Understanding how lucky I was, I realized, is what it meant to have wisdom.

By the time I memorized all thirty-five verses of Proverbs 3, I realized that I wasn't at rock bottom anymore.

I realized I was *content*.

A short time later, Oliver was stolen.

Everything changed after that. Everything I thought I knew, all the wisdom I thought I'd gained, went away. My heart was empty, and so was my life. Nothing made sense.

Nothing made sense.

And then I thought, *Did I just memorize a bunch of words that really mean nothing?*

That morning at my sister's house, I got up from the sofa and found Laura in the kitchen.

"Laura, I need to go back to Mount Vernon," I told her. "But I need to go alone. Just me. Someone knows more than they are saying. I need to go there by myself and find out."

Laura said she understood and wished me luck. I got in my car and set out for Mount Vernon all alone. But this time I brought something with me.

I brought Proverbs 3.

After all, I had memorized all the words, and now it was time for me to put those words into practice. It was time for me to demonstrate the proverb through my actions. "Have no fear of sudden disaster . . . ," it says, "for the LORD will be at your side and will keep your foot from being snared" (vv. 25–26).

This was now my new plan—to let love and forgiveness lead me back to Oliver.

I got to Mount Vernon and parked in front of the redbrick building on Norton Street. Outside it was cloudy and snowing and cold. I went into the building and up to the second floor. As I'd done the day before, I paused outside the door of 2W to catch my breath and steady myself. I had no idea what to expect, or how I'd be received. Would they slam the door in my face? Would I blame them if they did? After one last deep breath, I knocked.

The door opened, and the woman was there. I didn't even know her name. She seemed almost amused to see me.

"Oh, it's you," she said.

"Do you mind if I talk to you for a minute?" I said. "Just me and you."

She smiled. "Not at all," she said. "Come in."

An Oliver Story

When Oliver and I go for our walks and it's hot out, Oliver runs ahead of me until he finds a shady spot, then he lies down there and waits for me to catch up. When I reach him, he runs ahead again to find another shady spot. I can't say I blame him. If I had black fur like Oliver has, I'd want to spend as much time in the shade as possible.

   145

Chapter 20

Her name, I learned, was Donna. She looked to be around forty years old, and she was soft-spoken and had a kind, round face. Her apartment was cluttered with clothes and sneakers and toys. Donna's two young children, who had helped me look for Oliver the day before, were running around the living room, playing.

Before Donna could invite me in farther, I stood in the entrance hall and started talking.

"I just want to say that whoever took Oliver, I don't think they did it because they're a bad person," I said. "I think they just didn't understand my bond with Oliver. When he was taken, I was destroyed. I mean, *destroyed*. He took my heart. He took my *life*. The person who took Oliver *took my life*. And I think you understand that because you were out there yesterday helping me look for him. Now, I know Oliver isn't here. And I am not saying your son took him. But you need to know that I am not leaving this street until I find my dog. And I need to know if your son knows anything. So please, Donna, please—may I talk to your son?"

The emotions poured out. I was crying again. Even Donna wiped away a tear. She looked at me without a trace of anger and called over her youngest child.

"Go get Del," she told her.

The young girl ran to the back of the apartment and soon returned. A young man walked behind her. He was tall and thin, and he looked about seventeen. He had a handsome face, and he was wearing a baseball cap. He leaned against a wall in the living room and looked at me with no expression.

"This is Del," Donna said.

"Hi, Del. I'm Steven," I said. Del nodded but said nothing.

"I know they have been telling you my son did this, but they blame him for everything," Donna said.

"I understand," I said, looking at Del. "I'm not saying you took Oliver. I don't care if you did. All I care about is getting Oliver back. You gotta understand . . . you have to understand . . ."

I grasped for the right words as my heart broke open.

"Del, listen to me. I drive people to airports for a living. And I live with my dog. That's it. That's all I have. That's my life. So whoever took Oliver, they didn't just take my cell phone or my car or my computer. They took my whole life. You're looking at a broken man. And that's why I'm here. I need your help, Del. I'm asking you to help me find Oliver. Can you help me, please?"

Del looked down at his feet. It appeared to me like he was wiping away a tear of his own.

"Yes, I'll help," he said. "I'll make a couple of calls."

I was overcome by a feeling of gratitude. Gratitude for Donna and for her son Del and for her whole family.

Gratitude and affection and, above all, connection. Regardless of what came of this meeting, I realized the people in apartment 2W were not outsiders or strangers or enemies, as I'd once believed them to be. They were simply people with their own problems, some much worse than mine, struggling to make lives for themselves in challenging conditions. Donna was simply a mother trying to raise a family, and it wasn't always easy. It was often very hard, and yet she pushed on. And she did what she could to keep her family together.

And yet, despite their own hardships, they welcomed me into their home and listened to my story and offered to help me find Oliver. Even if it *was* Del who took Oliver—and I believed it was—they didn't have to let me into their apartment or help

They welcomed me, and they offered to help me.

me look for my dog. They could have shut me out and refused to talk to me at all. They could have treated me like an outsider, a stranger, the enemy. But they didn't. They welcomed me, and they offered to help me.

When I finally left apartment 2W and walked down the front stoop out into the cold air, I felt gratitude for Donna and her family but also something else. I felt—and this may sound strange—like my entire life had been preparing me and leading me to this very moment, on 328 Norton Street, in apartment 2W, with this family.

Suddenly, everything that had been confusing seemed clear. Why? Because in that moment, I had made an honest connection with someone who, only six days earlier, I had been so very angry with. This, I realized, was a gift. But it wasn't a gift bestowed on the kid in the baseball cap.

It was a gift bestowed on *me*.

I walked to the deli on the corner to get a cup of coffee. Then I called Laura to tell her how it went.

"They want to help us," I said. "They're going to help us."

Laura said she was coming down to Mount Vernon to join me. In about half an hour she pulled up and parked in front of the redbrick building. She stepped out of her car and gave me a big hug. I told her I believed that Del had some idea where Oliver was, and now he was going to go find him and bring him back.

All we can do is wait.

Five years old and sitting proudly with my mother.

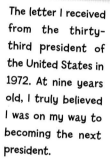

June 3, 1964, three days after my first birthday. My trademark crooked smile is already in place.

The letter I received from the thirty-third president of the United States in 1972. At nine years old, I truly believed I was on my way to becoming the next president.

THERE'S NOTHING BETTER THAN BEING WITH MY DAD.

The photo that started it all—snapped by Janice Connolly on the morning of February 19, 2019. By the time we arrived, Oliver was gone.

Reunited! The single greatest moment of my life came at noon on February 21, 2019.

Mickey, Gus, and Oliver.

A dapper Oliver is ready for his reception at Walaa's hair salon, Cleopatra, in Mount Vernon on March 2, 2019.

Isabela, Oliver, and Steven.

"All we can do is wait," I said.

Laura brought a bundle of newly printed flyers, and we walked around putting them up. Rolando, the mechanic, came out of his shop and saw us and waved.

"You won't leave, will you?" he said with a smile.

"Not without Oliver," I said.

A little later we ran into the two beat cops who had impounded the SUV. When they saw us, they smiled too.

"You guys again?" one of them said.

"We're not leaving," I said.

It was getting really cold out, so when we finished putting up flyers, we sat in Laura's car. There wasn't much for us to do but wait. Wait for Del or someone to contact us about Oliver. Now and then I'd get out of the car and walk around and look for Oliver, mostly just to stretch my legs. But for most of that day, Laura and I sat in her car and waited for something to happen.

A couple of hours in, I got a text alert on my phone.

Could this be it? I thought.

It wasn't. It was Helen, the young girl who was upset that Oliver got stolen and who had sent me a picture of her white Labrador to cheer me up.

Did you find Oliver yet?

Not yet. Keep your fingers crossed.

I will. Hang in there. You'll get him back.

The hours passed. Three o'clock. Four o'clock. Before I knew it, it was dark outside, and still no sign of Del or anyone who might have Oliver. The longer we waited, the harder it became for me to fight off the bad thoughts. Then it was 7:00 p.m., which meant I'd spent about ten hours in Mount Vernon, on Norton Street, just waiting. I searched the face of every person who walked down the block—man, woman, young, old—hoping to see some sign that they were involved in Oliver's theft. But there was nothing in their faces except indifference to my situation.

And then, around 8:00 p.m., a white car drove slowly past us and stopped about a car length in front. Laura and I watched with breaths held as the red brake lights came on.

Then, ever so slowly, the car began to back up.

It was like time stopped. Everything happened so slowly. The car kept rolling backward until it was alongside us. The windows were tinted, and it was too dark to see through them. *Is this it?* I thought. *Is Oliver in that car?*

Time stopped.

Finally, the car stopped, and the driver-side window came down. The driver was a young woman.

"Are you Oliver's father?" she asked.

Just then, a dog jumped onto the passenger seat and stuck his head out the window.

A small brown-and-black dog.

A dog that looked exactly like . . .

"Oliver!" I shouted.

I flung open my door and jumped out, hitting my head pretty hard on the doorframe. The quick movement startled the dog in the window, and he scampered out of view.

"Oliver?" I said. "Oliver, it's me!"

"Oh, no," the woman said. "This isn't Oliver. This is my little boy, Rocky."

Rocky? I thought. *Who's Rocky? What's going on? This dog looks exactly like Oliver!*

"I've been following your story on Facebook since Oliver got stolen," the woman explained. "I drove around all day looking for him. I'm so sorry for confusing you with Rocky."

I looked hard at her dog. Of course it wasn't Oliver. I could tell that now. He was sitting on his mother's lap, and he didn't want anything to do with me. I got back in Laura's car, my body trembling, my chest heavy and tight. The shock of seeing this nearly identical dog and believing for a moment that it was Oliver—it was devastating. *Devastating.* I looked at Laura, and I could tell she was feeling the same way. To be this close— *this close*—and still have no Oliver seemed like an impossibly cruel joke.

The woman apologized two or three more times, and I could tell she felt sincerely bad. She explained that she'd followed our story and decided to drive around Mount Vernon on a snowy night, Rocky in tow, hoping to spot Oliver and buy him from whoever had him. What kindness from a stranger!

I guess she just didn't anticipate our reaction to seeing Rocky. She couldn't have known how defeating this moment of false hope would be for us.

We thanked her for doing so much to help us, and after she left, we sat in Laura's car in silence. It was late and it was cold, and it was suddenly obvious to both of us that no one was coming anytime soon to hand over Oliver. What began as a promising day would end as just another sad X mark on the calendar. Six full days, and no Oliver.

"Let's go home," Laura said.

On the way to her house, a new thought popped into my head.

You know you're not getting Oliver back, Steven, don't you? I thought. *Surely you must know that by now.*

Chapter 21

It was only later that I learned what happened to Oliver. And when I learned it, I could imagine what Oliver had gone through and what he must have been thinking.

As he was taken out of my SUV on Valentine's Day and put in someone else's car, he would have thought, *Oh, no. This isn't good. This isn't good at all. Because the person who has me, the person who is taking me away, is not Stee.*

And when he found himself in a strange apartment in a strange building, with two young kids petting him and a mother arguing with her son, he would have behaved and thought, *Stee will come and get me. I just have to wait.*

He would have spent parts of five days in that apartment, with children who grew to love him and with a woman who fed him and gave him water and saw to it that he wasn't harmed. The rest of the time he would have been in the white SUV with the person who took him, the kid in the baseball cap, as the kid drove around and tried to sell him for $250. He wouldn't have understood what was happening, but he would have continued to play it cool.

Just bide your time. Don't bark or cry. Stee is on the way.

And then, on the fifth day, there would have been the commotion. The woman and the son standing beside the apartment's front windows, with their clear view of the street in front, watching as two police officers towed away the stolen white SUV. He would have heard the mother's hushed, angry words, and he would have felt two arms reach out to pick him up and hustle him to the back of the apartment.

He probably would have been really afraid.

This can't be good. Where is he taking me? Where is Stee? I need to see Stee!

And then, as the kid in the baseball cap climbed out of a back window and eased down the fire escape ladder with Oliver in one hand, jumping the last few feet to the ground of the courtyard, Oliver would have been really confused. Everything would have been moving too fast for him. Then he would have been left there, on a small patch of grass surrounded by dirt and trash and junk, in a tiny fenced-in courtyard in the back of the building, as the kid in the cap ran off somewhere so the cops wouldn't find him.

He would have sat there for a while, terrified, taking it in. The new smells, the new noises. After a while he would have gotten up and gingerly walked around, sniffing things, getting his bearings, his tail tucked down, his ears pinned back. He would have been on the alert for danger. He would have waited and listened—for what, he couldn't know.

And then, as more time passed with no activity around him, he would have kept moving, until he got to the broken chain link fence that separated the courtyard from the vacant lot next to the redbrick building. He would have carefully gone up to the fence and sniffed it. He would have seen the big hole at the bottom of the fence that left just enough room for him to squeeze through. And he would have thought, *Well, if Stee's not coming, then I guess I will go find Stee.*

Later that day, when the mother and her young children came looking for him and calling out his name, they would have found only an empty courtyard. And the next day, when the kid in the baseball cap began to try to find Oliver again, it really wouldn't have mattered, because by the time they started looking for him, Oliver was already long gone.

An Oliver Story

Oliver has a toughness to him. He knows how to get through a bad situation—say, for instance, walking in the rain. He doesn't love it, but he gets through it. I've always thought Oliver picked up that trait from me. I've learned how to grit my teeth and get through tough situations too. So I think my strength fed into Oliver and helped to make him the tough little critter he is. I guess you could say we feed off each other. We make each other better.

Chapter 22

*A*nd then two new people entered the story. These two people were born nine thousand miles away from Mount Vernon, in countries across from each other on the Red Sea.

Manny was raised in the country of Jordan, where his father owned a clothing factory. He was sixteen and knew just a little bit of English when his mother brought him to the United States to live with his aunt in Yonkers. Three of his siblings were already in the US because their parents believed they would have more opportunities there. Manny soon understood what they meant. Even in high school, he came to believe there was no career, no opportunity, that was off limits to him. He could do anything and be anyone he wanted. The sky was the limit. Because Manny liked the hustle and bustle of his father's clothing business, he knew his own future was to be a businessman.

When he was older, he rented a storefront in Mount Vernon and opened a deli. When the store next to his became available to rent, Manny snapped it up and expanded his deli. Some days he worked twenty hours or more, keeping his business successful while looking around for more and better opportunities.

It was around that time that, on an ordinary day, he drove to a nearby deli on Locust Street to visit a friend. On his way in, he happened to notice a woman standing a few yards away, on the corner of the block.

Wow, she is pretty, he thought. *Very pretty.*

Her name was Walaa, and she was born in Egypt to a big family of four sisters and two brothers. Her father passed away when she was young. She came to live in the United States with dreams of opening a hair salon.

She liked making people feel better about themselves.

Walaa first worked in a salon in Egypt when she was thirteen, and she found that she liked it. She liked making people feel better about themselves. She even had a name all picked out for her salon: Cleopatra. The Queen of Egypt, the ideal of all beauty.

Walaa settled in Mount Vernon. She found work in a salon on Locust Street and was taking a break and standing on the corner when she spotted a man looking at her from down the block. She looked away and looked back, and he was still there, looking at her.

He's very handsome, Walaa thought.

Over the next few weeks she would often notice the man standing outside the deli down the block, looking her way. Then one morning, when Walaa had a day off, she walked into a different deli—Manny's deli. To her surprise, the handsome man who looked at her from down the block was there.

Both Manny and Walaa were caught off guard, but they smiled at each other, as if to say, "Oh, it's you." They started talking, and the talk was easy and comfortable. They traded phone numbers and eventually went on a date. After that first date, they met and talked at least once a week about anything and everything, but mostly about their futures. Walaa told Manny about her plans for Cleopatra, while Manny shared his ambition to be the boss of a bunch of successful businesses.

One day over coffee, Manny got serious.

"So you're a good hairstylist, are you?" he asked.

"Yes, I am," Walaa replied.

"Well then, why don't we open a hair salon?"

Walaa looked to see if Manny was joking. But she already knew that he wasn't. One of the things she liked about him was that when he spoke about the future, he was very serious about it. Manny was determined to succeed, and Walaa liked that, because she was determined too.

"If you leave the salon and come work with me, we'll open your salon in the store next door to the deli," Manny went on. "Look, we both know what we want. We have the same goals. We want to be successful. We want to get married. We want big families. So—let's do it together."

A more formal proposal soon followed. But from that day forward, Manny and Walaa were as together as any two people could be.

They got married, had two sons, and followed their dreams. They sold their two cars to help finance the salon and couldn't afford a car of their own, so they had to borrow Manny's sister's 2006 Honda van to get around. All the money they earned they put straight into their new joint business venture: Cleopatra's Hair Salon.

After weeks of working on the interior—new wood floors, gold-painted walls and ceiling, black leather chairs, elegant chandeliers—Manny and Walaa were almost ready for the grand opening. Every detail was perfect, down to the red, white, and blue balloons. Just a few last-minute fixes remained before the official opening in three short days.

On the morning of Tuesday, February 19, Manny dropped Walaa off at Cleopatra's, then drove up Francisco Street and turned right at the gas station onto Garfield Avenue. Manny was on his way to pick up some supplies for the salon. As soon as he turned onto Garfield, he saw a big black rat trudging slowly across the avenue, straight into traffic, a few feet in front of his van.

Manny hit the brakes and watched the rat go by. As he looked closer, he could tell it wasn't a rat. No, it was a cat.

Then he noticed the thing had a fluffy tail, and its tail was tucked down as it slouched slowly across the busy avenue.

That's not a cat, Manny thought. *That's a dog.*

Manny put the van in park and jumped out and went over to the dog.

"Hey, buddy," Manny said. "Are you lost?"

Oliver's Thoughts

I'm really confused and scared. I don't know where I am. I thought I could find Stee! Who is this man? I think I'll go to him. Maybe he can help me find Stee.

The dog stopped, turned, and slowly walked toward Manny. Manny reached down and picked him up. He looked him over more closely. Other than a layer of dirt, he didn't look too bad off. He wasn't hurt or bleeding or anything.

There was nothing about him that made Manny think he was a stray dog. In fact, Manny concluded, the opposite was true.

This is somebody's dog, he thought. *Somebody loves this dog.*

Just then, a car drove by and stopped. The driver stuck his head out the window.

"You just find that dog?"

"Yeah," Manny said.

"If you don't want him, I'll take him," the man said.

Manny stood there with the dog in his arms, considering the offer. He and Walaa were way too busy to add a dog to their lives. Maybe they'd get one down the road, but certainly not right then. There couldn't have been a worse time for them to take on that kind of responsibility. Manny could just give the dog to this stranger and be done with it.

Manny looked at the dog again. The dog peered up at him with big, innocent eyes.

Oliver's Thoughts

Please don't give me to anyone else. Please! I'll be good. I promise. I'll behave just as Stee taught me to. Even if I never see Stee again, I'll behave—just don't give me to anyone else. You seem like a nice man. I trust you.

Maybe his owner is looking for him, Manny thought. *Maybe we won't have to keep him forever.*

"Nah, don't worry about it," Manny told the driver. "I'll hold on to him."

An Oliver Story

When I take Oliver to the car wash, he sees me vacuuming out the car, and he barks and wags his tail and playfully nips at the vacuum. People walk by and see him wrestling with the vacuum, and they say, "Hey, what is your dog doing?" And I say, "What's it look like? He's attacking the vacuum!" Then they laugh and walk away.

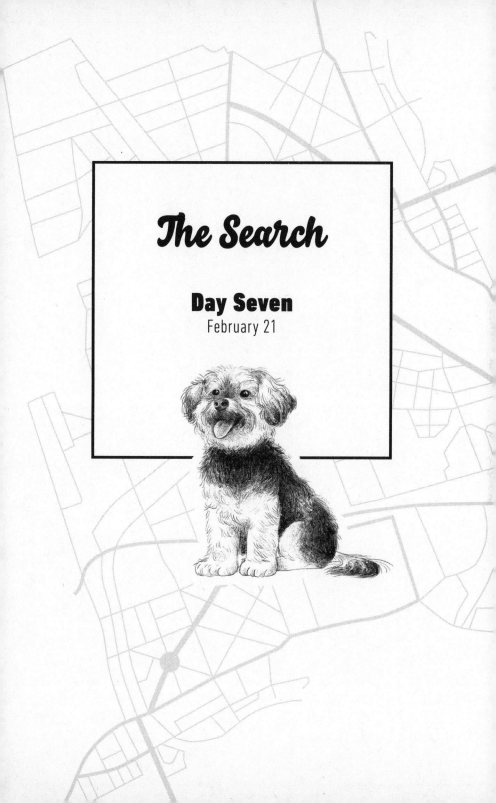

The Search

Day Seven
February 21

Chapter 23

I spent the night on Laura's sofa and woke up after nine solid hours of sleep. It was probably the best sleep I'd had since Oliver was stolen. I guess I was exhausted. The days were blending into each other, and I didn't even realize that Thursday marked one full week since Oliver had been taken.

The day before in Mount Vernon had been hard. Seeing the look-alike Oliver crushed our spirits. The worst part for me was feeling for the first time that Laura was also starting to question why we hadn't gotten Oliver back.

She was my rock, but even she felt punched in the gut by what happened the day before. The longer we went without Oliver, the harder it would be for either of us to pretend we believed we would get him back.

I got a cup of coffee from the kitchen and checked Nancy's Facebook page about Oliver. For a guy who wasn't really into

Facebook, I'd sure found it a source of comfort there as I read people's comments and well wishes.

There were hundreds of them. I checked the number of shares and likes, which had been growing steadily all week.

We were now over fifteen thousand.

I signed off of Facebook and told Laura I was going back to Mount Vernon. She said she was coming with me. Nancy had the day off from work, and she called to say she would meet us there too.

Maybe, just maybe, this could be the day.

"I don't want you two to be there alone," she said. "I cannot sit here and do nothing."

We had no plan for the day. All we could really do once we got there was sit and wait. But even so, driving down the Bronx River Parkway to Mount Vernon, on a day when bright sunshine replaced the dreary clouds, I had an inkling, a tiny hint, the very beginnings of a feeling that maybe, just maybe, this could be the day.

On the drive down, I suddenly remembered a moment I had with my father a long time ago.

Like I said, my father could be a really great dad, but he could also be mean. He could say hurtful things. It was almost like he just couldn't help it. Sometimes I thought that if my father hadn't been so hard on me on his bad days, maybe I'd have grown up to be a different person. Of course, that was something I would never really know.

I remembered a day when my father and I went to the supermarket. My father was sixty-six years old, and he was kind of sick. He was pushing the shopping cart and coughing and moving slowly. The night before, he had been in one of his bad moods and had said something mean to me. I can't even remember what it was. I hadn't fought back—I'd stopped fighting back long ago. I'd learned to just walk away.

The next morning Dad and I went shopping. A few feet from the entrance to the supermarket, my father suddenly stopped. He turned and looked at me.

"Steven, I'm sorry for what I said last night," he said.

"It's okay, Dad."

"No, it's *not*," he said forcefully, grabbing my arm and gripping it tightly. "It's not okay."

He let go of my arm and looked away.

"I don't know why I do what I do," he said. "But it's not right. I just don't know why I do it. But I'm sorry I hurt you so much. I'm really sorry, Steven."

Why did my father do the things he did? That was something else I would never know. But there was something about my father's apology—the first time he'd ever apologized for his actions—that really got to me. It was like a curtain was pulled back and I finally saw my father for who he was—a human being, just like me, who was trying to do the best he could. And

I realized that, while he loved his family very much, I'm not so sure how much he loved himself.

I finally saw my father for who he was—a human being, just like me.

In any case, my father could never change the past, and neither could I. All we have is the present, the now. And when my father apologized to me, I was able to completely forgive him, not just for the night before but for *everything* he ever said or did. All I felt for him was love.

I put my hand on my father's shoulder and told him again that it was okay. We were good. We were fine. Everything was fine. Then we went into the supermarket, my father moving slowly and coughing, and we picked up some groceries and went home.

My father passed away a few months later. Since his passing, I have visited him and my mother at St. Patrick's Cemetery in Huntington hundreds of times, just to talk to them and ask for their help, to let my mother know that I am doing okay, and to thank my father for the day he taught me the awesome power of forgiveness.

Chapter 24

Manny put the scruffy dog in the passenger seat of his sister's Honda van, turned around, and headed back to Cleopatra's. The dog immediately jumped on his lap and put his face to the window. Manny lowered the window, and the dog stuck part of his head out, enjoying the sharp, cold wind on his face.

Oliver's Thoughts

Wow, this is nice! This reminds me of driving with Stee. Maybe he is taking me to him. Maybe he is taking me to Stee! I am going to be on my best behavior with him.

Okay, this dog is car-friendly, Manny thought. *For sure he's a dog who lives in a home. Someone owns this dog.*

Manny double-parked outside the hair salon and walked

inside with the dog. Walaa looked up from what she was doing, and her mouth dropped open.

"What is that?" she asked.

"This is somebody's dog," Manny said. "I found him on Garfield Avenue. Somebody treated him well and really loves him, I can tell. But he's lost, and he's really sad."

"Okay," Walaa said, "let's put him on the chair in the back. I have a customer coming. I hope he doesn't bark."

Manny put the dog on the brown leather chair, and the dog sat there quietly and looked around.

"He must be hungry," Manny said before going to a deli and picking up a quarter pound of smoked turkey. Back at the salon, he put the turkey on a paper plate and poured water into a cup. Then he put the plate and cup on a chair next to the sofa. The dog came over and ate all the turkey and drank all the water. Then he looked up at Manny and Walaa and licked his lips as if to say thank you.

Oliver's Thoughts

You know what? You humans are really kind. Everyone! You don't even know me, but you're so nice to me. I need kindness right now because I still miss Stee.

Manny remembered something someone had told him—if you feed a dog once, he will remember you for three years. He didn't know if that was true, but he felt he had earned the little dog's trust, and that made him feel good.

"Buddy, you're gonna be just fine," he told the dog.

That evening Manny and Walaa took the dog home with them to their apartment a few blocks away. They had a new baby, two-month-old Ameer, and it was a hectic time, even before the dog showed up. But what could they do now but take care of him until his rightful owner showed up?

That night Walaa mixed some wet and dry dog food and put it on a dish on the floor of their bedroom, where their two sons were lying on the bed. Meanwhile, Manny went to another room to change out of his work clothes.

When he returned, he saw the dog up on the bed, happily lying next to their two children.

"Maybe we should give him a bath," Walaa said.

Oliver's Thoughts

Stee was funny when he would give me a bath. He would tell me to sit still, so I would frolic more just to watch him get playfully angry. He was so funny!

I get sad sometimes, even during this nice bath with this nice person. But I will do what Stee taught me. Be cool and behave. After all, this is a really nice family.

Manny took the dog to the bathroom and washed him in the tub. The dog didn't resist a bit. He wasn't too dirty, but he did have a smell to him. Manny took him out of the tub and tried to dry him with a towel. But he was still wet, so Manny used his wife's hairdryer to gently blow him dry.

When he put the clean dog on the floor, the dog ran straight back to the bedroom and jumped on the bed again.

"He wants to be with the kids," Walaa said.

Oliver's Thoughts

I feel so refreshed! These little kids are cute! I hope the woman lets me sleep on the bed with her and the kids. I could cuddle right up to her.

The dog was so quiet and well-mannered and loveable that Manny and Walaa were both smitten pretty quickly. Before long, it would occur to both Manny and Walaa that if the dog's owner never showed up, well, that might not be the worst thing that could happen.

"Honey," Walaa told Manny, "I think he wants to sleep in here."

Manny knew what that meant. He grabbed his pillow, let the dog have his spot in the bed, and slept on the sofa that night.

Two days later, on the morning of Thursday, February 21, Manny and Walaa got ready to leave for work at 9:00 a.m. Nobody had come to claim the dog, but that was okay with them because the dog had been no problem at all. That morning, though, as they were leaving, the dog raced toward them and got between them and the door and started yelping, which so far he hadn't done.

"What is it, buddy?" Manny asked. "What's wrong?"

The dog kept barking, and Manny thought he knew what the dog was trying to say.

He was saying, *I wanna go! Don't leave me here! Take me with you today, please.*

"He wants to come with us," Walaa told Manny.

> Take me with you today, please.

"Well, then, I guess he gets to come," Manny said.

They decided to take the dog with them on an errand and then back to the salon, where he could spend the day with Walaa. Manny got the van, and as Walaa loaded up the boys, the dog jumped into Manny's lap in the driver's seat.

Manny rolled down the window, and the dog stuck out its head. *How about that,* Manny thought. *We already have a ritual.*

Manny drove the van to the depot, where he picked up more supplies. Then they went back to the salon. It was midmorning, and the traffic was heavy. To avoid a jam on the route he normally took, Manny turned down Cresswell Boulevard, toward Norton Street. As he headed to the corner, he saw the traffic light ahead turn yellow. He punched the gas and tried to beat the red light. He almost made it, but at the last second, he had to hit the brakes. The van sat at the corner of Norton and Cresswell, waiting for a green light.

"Manny, look at that," Walaa said suddenly.

"Look at what?"

"That, up there. That paper on the pole."

Manny looked out his window. On the corner he saw a telephone pole, and taped to the pole was a piece of paper.

Some kind of flyer.

On the flyer he saw a picture of a dog.

Chapter 25

*W*hen we got to Mount Vernon, Laura and I walked around handing out flyers. Neither of us was feeling all that positive. As we were walking around, two police officers in a squad car pulled up alongside us.

"You guys again?" one of them said.

It was the same two officers who had impounded the stolen SUV. They were both smiling, apparently surprised to see us still in Mount Vernon, still searching for Oliver.

"We're not leaving without my dog," I told them. They both smiled.

"You're gonna be able to run for mayor of this town if you keep walking the streets every day," one of the officers said with a laugh. "Just be careful."

They drove off, and Laura and I sat in her car, which we parked outside the redbrick building. Not much later, Nancy arrived from Brooklyn and joined us in the car.

There wasn't much for us to do but wait. Wait for something good to happen. During the last few days we'd never given a thought to when or where we would eat. We just grabbed food when we could, usually at the end of a long day. This wasn't the healthiest thing to do, so I asked my sisters if they were hungry. They said they were. For once, we were going to have something resembling a proper breakfast.

I walked to the corner deli and ordered three egg sandwiches and three coffees. The woman behind the counter looked at me and asked, "Hey, you're the guy with the stolen dog, right?" I told her that I was.

"Well, I really hope you find him soon."

I smiled and thanked her and paid for the food.

"You know what?" I said before leaving. "This is a really wonderful community. Really nice people."

"We have a bad reputation," she said. "But once you're in the community, you see that everyone's got your back."

I carried the food back to where we were parked. In Laura's car we tore into our sandwiches, which were delicious. The top of Laura's dashboard was soon covered with wrappings, coffee cup lids, stirrers, and napkins.

"We're like detectives," I said.

"Yeah, detectives on a stakeout," Laura said.

Suddenly, my cell phone chimed. The number was unfamiliar. Over the week I'd received a number of calls that turned out to be either well-wishers or false leads, so I no longer got excited by calls.

It was a little before noon when I answered the phone. "Hello?"

"Hello, is this Steven?"

"Yes, I'm Steven. Who is this?"

"My name is Manny. I'm calling to see, uh . . . are you missing a dog?"

At the corner of Norton and Cresswell Boulevard, Manny stepped out of his sister's van to get a closer look at the flyer on the telephone pole. He pulled it down from the pole and took it back to the van.

"I think it's him," he told Walaa.

The dog was now snuggled on Walaa's lap, and she was holding him tightly.

Oliver's Thoughts

Something is going on. Why did they stop? Are they getting rid of me too? Oh no, I like these people. Please don't get rid of me.

"How do you know?"

"I don't know, but it looks like him."

"Yeah, but it might not be him. We can't just hand him over to anybody."

"The only way to know is to call the guy. Let me call the guy."

Manny pulled the van into a parking spot. He took out his cell and entered the number on the flyer. After two rings, someone picked up.

"Hello, is this Steven?" he asked.

When the guy on the phone asked me if I was Steven, I told him that I was and waited to hear what he had to say.

"I have a dog right here," he said. "He's black and brown, like the dog in the photo. I don't know, it kinda looks like him."

"Who is it?" I heard Laura ask.

"Shhhh," I told her. "It's some guy who says he might have Oliver."

Suddenly, I heard barking come over the phone.

Wait a minute, I thought. *I think I know that bark.*

On the phone Manny heard a female voice ask who was calling, and then he heard the man use the name Oliver.

Suddenly, the dog in Walaa's lap started barking.

Barking loudly.

"Wait a minute," Manny said. "Is that your dog's name? Oliver? That's his name?"

"Yes, that's his name. His name is Oliver."

"Okay, wait a minute. Let me try something."

Manny turned to the little dog on Walaa's lap. The dog looked back with big wide eyes.

"Oliver?" Manny said to the dog. "Are you Oliver?"

Oliver's Thoughts

My name! My name! How do you know my name? What's going on? What's happening? Let me up! Why are you saying my name?

The dog jumped up and down and wagged his tail and barked and spun in a circle and otherwise went dog crazy.

Manny looked at Walaa. Now they knew.

It was the first time Oliver had heard his name in a week.

"Listen, I think I have your dog," the man on the phone told me. "I said his name, and he is going nuts."

The sensation that came over me in that instant was a mix of joy and disbelief. I felt shot through with adrenaline, and nothing seemed real. I had to force myself to be in the moment and not get ahead of myself.

"Where are you?" I nearly shouted into the phone.

"We're headed toward North MacQuesten Parkway."

"What? Where is that? How do you spell it?"

Nancy and Laura searched frantically for a pen. They couldn't find one. The half-eaten sandwiches were spilling everywhere.

"Who is he? What's he saying?" Laura asked.

"Shhh, I can't hear him."

"Put the call on speaker," said Laura. I put the call on speaker.

"Hold on, let me FaceTime you," the guy on the phone said. "I'll put the dog on camera if I can get him to sit still."

I switched to FaceTime and stared at the phone. A man came into view. The image blurred as he moved the phone around. Finally, it stabilized, and a dog was in the frame. The dog was sitting on a woman's lap. I looked at the dog and blinked three or four times. Time stopped.

"That's him!" I shouted. "That's Oliver! It's him, it's him, it's Oliver!"

"Let me see! Let me look," my sisters said. I handed my phone to Laura.

"Tell me it's him," I said. "Tell me it's him. Is that him?"

"It looks like him," Laura said.

"Nancy, is it him? Tell me it's him!"

"It could be him," Nancy said. "It really looks like him."

"It's Oliver, right? It's him. Is it him?"

Both Laura and Nancy reached their conclusions at the same time.

"That's Oliver," they both said.

They handed me the phone, and I looked at the dog again. I locked eyes with the dog. Oliver is one of those dogs who can read screens well. He always recognizes dogs on TV. Could he see me through the iPhone screen and understand it was me? Could he recognize me this way?

I will never know for sure, but as we looked at each other through the tiny screen, I truly believed he was thinking, *There's Stee! There's Stee! I knew he was coming! I knew it!*

"That's Oliver!" I screamed at the man on the phone. "That's my Oliver! Where are you? Where are you *right now*?"

Oliver's Thoughts

That's Stee! I know his voice! That's Stee! Where is he? Where is he? That's my daddy!

Manny said, "Hold on, let me look around."

There was a pause, and then he came back on the call. "I'm on Cresswell Boulevard," he said.

"I know where Cresswell Boulevard is!" I said. "It's right down the block from me. I'm looking at it right now!"

"Wait a minute, so you're right here?" Manny said.

"Do me a favor. Hold up your phone," I said. "Hold it up in the air."

Manny held up the phone and let me see the store on the corner—a door, a window, and a place called the Blue Raccoon. The store's sign featured two images of blue raccoons. I saw the two raccoons, and I recognized them immediately. I knew I had seen them before. I had walked by that sign during the last week. In fact, I knew exactly where it was.

It was at the end of the very block where I was sitting. "You're down the street!" I yelled into the phone. "You're right here! Nancy, Laura, he's right down the block. Oliver is right down the block!"

To Manny, I yelled, "Stay where you are!"

I jumped out of Laura's car, my egg sandwich and coffee jumping out with me and spilling to the curb. My sisters and I were a flurry of arms and legs. I didn't wait for them—I took off running down the block. If a man can fly, well then, I believe I flew down that street. For a brief moment in my fifty-five years of living, I was finally the baseball hero rounding third base in game seven of the World Series, bursting with speed, madly dashing for victory, the crowd cheering for me to "Run!"

For a few brief seconds I had wings, and my feet barely touched the ground.

As I neared the corner of Norton, I strained to see Manny or Oliver. All I could see was a big blue van. It was parked on the corner, across the street from the Blue Raccoon. I ran to the van, completely out of breath. And then I felt my knees nearly give out.

Because the passenger side door of the van was open, and a woman was sitting inside the van, and on her lap was my sweet, wonderful, beautiful boy.

Oliver!

Oliver's Thoughts

STEE! I knew it! I knew it! You're here! Where were you? My heart is beating so fast. I love you, Daddy! I love you!

He jumped from Walaa's lap straight into my arms. I held him and staggered backward and fell against the chain link fence, and I let my body slump to the sidewalk. I squeezed Oliver and buried my face in his hair and cried. My crying was loud and shrill. Laura and Nancy came around the corner shouting Oliver's name. I didn't want to let go of him, but I knew he had to breathe, so I loosened my grip—and he wiggled away and shook his body and jumped right back in my arms. I sat up against the fence and cradled Oliver and just stared at him. I felt myself return to the land of the living. I felt my life go from black and white to color. I held my little warm ball of life, and I felt my mother and father there on the sidewalk with me in this moment of victory, just as they had been in my time of defeat.

I felt God lift me up, so I could finally stand.

Oliver was home. Oliver was home. Oliver was home.

Chapter 26

In the next hour or so, the corner of Norton and Cresswell became a busy place. Two women in a car drove by, and when they saw me sitting on the sidewalk with Oliver, they screeched to a stop.

"Is that Oliver?" one of them yelled.

"Yes, I got him back!"

"Oh my goodness, I can't believe it! We've been following your story! We're so happy for you!"

Next, a woman we spoke to on Norton Street three days earlier, Gina, walked past. Gina's friendliness early on had really lifted our spirits and set the tone for the kindness we found in Mount Vernon. Now she got to see the incredible reunion for herself.

"God bless you," she said, tears in her eyes. "God bless you and Oliver."

Two more women came running out of the store on the corner. They'd been following the story too, and they started crying as well. Two days earlier, four young teenagers had helped us search the neighborhood for Oliver. They walked by the corner and stopped to celebrate, whooping and high-fiving each other. Even the two police officers we met on our first day in Mount Vernon walked over to see what the commotion was about and stuck around and posed for pictures with us. They were smiling as widely as everyone else.

"I told you I wasn't leaving until we got him!" I told them.

It was a spontaneous outpouring of love, support, and happiness. Cars driving by honked their horns, and nearly every person who passed had heard of Oliver and stopped to say hello. Laura called Lisa Reyes at News 12, and within an hour they had a crew at the scene. We filmed the happy resolution to our story. Manny and Walaa were interviewed and described their remarkable role in rescuing Oliver.

I didn't let Oliver out of my arms.

In all that time I didn't let Oliver out of my arms. Nor did he wiggle or squirm or otherwise ask to be let down.

Neither of us was in any hurry to be separated again, even by just a few feet.

The commotion finally died down, and I hugged Manny and Walaa and thanked them profusely for what they had done. I made sure to get their phone numbers and told them I would return soon because I wanted to give them some of the reward money. Then Laura, Nancy, and I walked back to the car. I noticed Terry and Rolando outside their shop. I went over to show them Oliver and gave them each $200 for their help.

"I'm very happy for you, brother," Rolando said.

Then I noticed a woman looking down at us through the window of her apartment in the redbrick building.

It was Donna. When she saw me with Oliver, she smiled.

"I'm very happy for you," she yelled down to me. I felt my eyes well up with tears.

"Thank you," I said. "Thank you for everything. Good luck to you. We are going home now."

There was a reason why all of this happened.

We have to trust that when something happens, it happens for a reason, Lucy's husband, Alan, had said. He was right. There *was* a reason why all of this happened. You see, the world is more mysterious, and more miraculous, than we can ever know.

The three of us drove to Laura's house and threw ourselves a little party. My friend Eric and his girlfriend, Lisa, came over to share in the celebration. I examined Oliver from head to toe, looking for injuries, and he seemed perfectly fine. Manny and Walaa had obviously treated him well, and so had Del and his family. In Laura's living room I put Oliver on the floor to try and gauge his mental state. Would he run and hide? Would he flinch? Would he seem afraid?

A dog toy Oliver liked to play with at Laura's house was on the floor by the sofa.

"Oliver, go get your toy!" I said. "Go get it."

Oliver pranced straight to the toy and brought it over, his movements as familiar to me as my own. We were picking up right where we left off.

> We were picking up right where we left off.

Every few minutes one of us would say how we couldn't believe Oliver was there with us. Even when I had Oliver on my lap, part of me couldn't accept that he was actually back.

It had been so, so long since I'd held him or even looked at his face, and now that he was with me, it didn't seem real. I had to give Oliver a little squeeze now and then just to make sure he wouldn't disappear in a puff of smoke.

Nancy updated her Facebook page with the good news. By then, her post had been seen by nearly *ninety thousand* people! Not much later, I got a text message. It was from Helen, the young girl in Iowa who'd cried when Oliver was taken.

> I heard you got Oliver back! Congratulations!
> I'm so happy for you both!

I took a picture of Oliver and me on Laura's sofa and sent it to her, thanking her for being there to comfort me in one of the darkest moments of my life.

Then I sent the same picture of Oliver and me to Isabela, the young woman whose wisdom changed my life the night I drove her to Bard College in the snow.

> We got him back!

> I am SO happy for you!

I made a bunch of calls that day. To my friend Tony. To my uncle Pat. To Lucy and Alan. To everyone who stepped forward out of love and kindness and literally kept me from collapsing in a heap. When I finally had a free moment, I took Oliver out to Laura's backyard, and I thanked my mother and father and brother up in heaven.

And then I told God that I was grateful to Him.

When Oliver was stolen, the horror and misery of his loss sent me back to my old way of thinking—that God had let me down, that this was my destiny as a Carino, that I would never see Oliver again. Here was my chance to put Proverbs 3 into practice—after weeks and weeks of memorizing it on my walks with Oliver—and instead I had disregarded it.

"Trust in the LORD with all your heart and lean not on your own understanding," the proverb says (v. 5). Instead, I leaned on my old beliefs about who I was and the world around me.

But my ordeal lasted for seven days, and in that time, things changed. In that time I was given many gifts—the gift of kindness, of community, of love. Many different people from all walks of life crossed my path and changed my way of thinking. Friends reminded me I was loved; strangers shared my pain. A single block in a challenged neighborhood became my world, and I saw that this world was beautiful. Words of wisdom came from everywhere, filling my heart.

And in the end, the hatred and resentment I was harboring disappeared, replaced by love and compassion. Distrust gave way to trust. This is what I thanked God for in Laura's backyard—not for returning Oliver to me but for putting me through the trial of my life and giving me the wisdom to get through it.

That night I curled up on Laura's sofa, and Oliver jumped up and snuggled next to me, in the hollow between my legs and my arms, and we both fell fast asleep and didn't wake up until long after the sun came up.

Oliver's Thoughts

This is where I always want to sleep. Thank you, Daddy, for never giving up on me, because I never gave up on you.

Chapter 27

A few days later Oliver and I were back in Mount Vernon.

The occasion was a party to celebrate the happy ending to our story. The place was Cleopatra's Hair Salon, which was now proudly open to the public.

It was Nancy's suggestion to have a party there, and Manny and Walaa happily agreed. They were both really moved by the roles they played in returning Oliver to me, and they wanted to be part of the celebration. We expected ten or twelve people to show up. More than forty people wound up coming.

It was an amazing event. My sisters were there, along with some of their friends who had followed the story. My pals Eric and Tony showed up, and Lucy and Alan, and Janice Connolly. Some Mount Vernon residents popped in to say hello, and even some Facebook friends stopped by. So many people brought lovely little presents for Oliver. The mayor of Mount Vernon, who heard about our story, arrived and stayed for a long while, happy to talk about the kind, caring people of his city. Oliver ran around the salon and munched on some of the food we set out. He sat in a few laps and acted thrilled to be around so many people who knew his name and beamed at the sight of him.

At some point I picked up Oliver and stood at the top of the small staircase at the back of Cleopatra's, looking down over the crowd. Then I gave a little speech. I thanked everyone for coming, and I gave a brief description of the events of the week. I talked about all the beautiful people I met in Mount Vernon and the many ways my time in the community had changed me. And I talked about what my friend Eric told me when I was really down—that I was like George Bailey from *It's a Wonderful Life.*

"George Bailey got to see what life would have been like if he hadn't been born," I said. "I got to see what my life would be like without Oliver. But I also got to see how loved I am. I was given the gift of witnessing the love and support of my family, friends, clients, strangers, and of course, the citizens of Mount Vernon. And I am extremely grateful for that. I feel the same way George Bailey felt at the end of the movie. I feel like I am the richest man in town."

> I got to see how loved I am.

A few days before the event, I came back to Mount Vernon to hand out the reward money. I divided it between Janice Connolly, who first spotted Oliver and called me, and Manny and Walaa, who brought him back to me. They all refused to accept it at first, but I insisted.

Then, at Cleopatra's during the party, Walaa came over and asked me to walk with her to the front of the salon. We stood by the big window, and Walaa pointed at something out on the street. I saw a bright-red Jeep parked in front of the salon.

"That is what you did for us, Steven," she said.

Manny and Walaa had used the reward money I gave them to finally get their own car, a used but shiny red Jeep.

I started to tear up again, as I had a few times that day. The love and affection I felt in that room

To be given, in essence, a new life in the world seemed like an extraordinary blessing.

were overwhelming. For a long time I'd had a solitary existence in my little one-room cottage. Now, to feel such a warm embrace from so many people—to be given, in essence, a new life in the world—seemed like an extraordinary blessing. I found I didn't have the words to properly express the gratitude I felt, so instead I just cried a lot.

I guess I could say life returned to normal for Oliver and me, but that wouldn't really be true. For me, nothing was normal

195

> The world around me hadn't changed, but the way I looked at it had.

again, or at least not the "normal" I knew. I felt like I'd been transformed by what happened over those seven days in February. The world around me hadn't changed, but the way I looked at it had.

As the days passed, I thought less and less about the actual events of that week—the false leads and crushing setbacks, the lucky coincidences, all the things that had to go right for me to get Oliver back. But one thought above all kept pushing its way back in my mind, and after a while I could no longer ignore it.

So two weeks after finding Oliver, I bundled him into my car, and together we went back to Mount Vernon.

You see, I'd been thinking a lot about the kid in the baseball cap.

I really didn't know much about him, other than that he had a bad rap in the neighborhood. I knew his mother was struggling to keep him on the straight and narrow. I also knew he created the worst crisis of my adult life.

But then I began to wonder, had he also created his *own* worst crisis that week? Was stealing Oliver routine and easy for him, or had he crossed some kind of line? Perhaps Del had taken Oliver to give to his mother as a Valentine's Day gift, which would mean that he had a good heart. I also suspected he'd grown to like Oliver, and that, too, gave me a glimpse of his humanity. What if that week had been a turning point for him? What if, like me, he drew some valuable life lessons from what had happened?

Del, the kid in the baseball cap, came into my life and without realizing it played a huge part in my transformation.

But what if I was also supposed to play a part in his?

When we first spoke in his apartment, Del gave me his email address, and a few days after getting Oliver back, I sent him an email. I told him I hoped we might be able to get together and just talk. I had no idea what I would say to him if we did meet; basically, I was following my gut. But the email bounced back to me. I sent him a few more, and they all bounced back. I figured he'd given me a phony email, which left me only one choice if I wanted to see him.

Go back to Norton Street.

I took the Hutchinson River Parkway from Bedford to Mount Vernon and headed straight for the redbrick building. I found a parking spot across from it, and I picked up Oliver and went out for a walk on the block. I was hoping I'd run into Del, but he never appeared. I didn't want to go up to his apartment and bother his family again; I was just hoping to bump into him. Something told me I was going to see him that day. So Oliver and I went back to the redbrick building, and we sat together on the front stoop.

Within minutes, Del walked out.

He saw me and broke into a big smile. Then he saw Oliver and reached down and gently patted him on the head.

"Hi, Oliver," he said.

"Del, it's good to see you," I told him. "I was trying to reach you. I sent you emails, but they all bounced back."

"Oh, yeah?" he said. "That's funny. It should be working."

"Okay," I said. "I'll try again."

"Yeah, try again."

"So how are you doing, Del?"

"I'm good. I'm okay."

"That's good to hear because I really wanted to know how you were doing."

Then we fell into silence. I didn't know what more to say; I didn't even know what I was doing there. What was my plan?

Weren't we both a part of the special community created by Oliver?

What had I expected? Del and I were from two different worlds. We couldn't know each other's lives or experiences. We weren't close in age, and we didn't live in the same place. We weren't part of the same community.

Or were we?

Weren't we both a part of the special community created by Oliver?

"I gotta go," Del finally said.

"Listen, before you go—I just, I just wanted us to talk," I said. "Just talk sometime, you know?"

"Okay," he said.

"Okay then. I'll email you again. And maybe we can get together sometime."

Del smiled and shook my hand. Then he started walking away.

A few steps down the street, he turned and gave Oliver and me a little wave.

"Talk to you later," he said.

"Yeah, definitely, talk later," I said.

And I meant it. I knew right then that I would see Del again, and I knew what I wanted to do for him. If he would allow me, I wanted to take him to an animal rescue and get him his own dog. Maybe he would say no. Maybe he hadn't really fallen in love with Oliver like I suspected. But something told me he might say yes. And if he did, then he'd come to realize what I already knew—dogs make us better humans. They bring out the best in us.

Conclusion

Our first night back at the cottage together, I took all of Oliver's toys out of the closet and scattered them all over the floor so he could play with them. I sat in the chair and watched him toss around his favorite little rubber elephant, and I tried to imagine what he was thinking when, after seven days apart, he saw me on that street in Mount Vernon.

That's him! he would have thought. *That's my dad! I knew he wouldn't forget me. I knew he would come get me.*

Oliver stopped playing for a moment and looked up at me and, well, I know dogs can't really smile, but I could swear that Oliver smiled at me. Like I said, I believe Oliver and I understand each other's thoughts. And what we were both thinking was, *It's really good to see you again.*

That was sort of the same way I felt about God. The same week I lost Oliver, I also experienced a loss of my connection with God. I felt abandoned by Him. But I was wrong. God never abandoned me. He was always right there with me. He tried to tell me this through Proverbs 3: "Trust in the LORD with all your heart and lean not on your own understanding" (v. 5). I thought I'd absorbed the lesson, but really I hadn't.

So He taught it to me again in Mount Vernon.

I don't know what the future holds for Oliver or for Del or for me. Will there be more hardships and setbacks? Probably. To be alive means we face tests all the time. Going forward, will I be able to see these tests as opportunities to show love and compassion and, as my father taught me, forgiveness? I sure hope I will.

What I do know for certain is that we are all part of a community. Geographic communities, spiritual communities, even accidental communities—there is always something that binds us to each other. Which means that none of us is ever truly alone. I believe this now.

It's written on the tablet of my heart.

Acknowledgments

The story of Oliver is a gift. It is a true story about the power of faith. To the young reader, always believe in yourself and your abilities. Everything you will ever need resides in your heart.

I would like to first acknowledge the power of faith, which is to give thanks to God, my parents, and my brother, Frank. Thank you for restoring my life and somehow helping all of us get Oliver back to me. So, to those who we cannot see, thank you for giving me the two most important virtues a person could ask for, wisdom and understanding.

To begin with, I must thank quite a few people who made this story possible. First is my cowriter, Alex Tresniowski. Your talent and skill as a heartfelt writer are second to none. You have taken my story, my words, and made them beautiful and emotional. It has been an honor to be associated with you on this book.

Where would I be without my sisters? Laura, to say you came to the aid of your little brother is an understatement. Your determination to get Oliver back was incredible. Thank you for never giving up on Oliver or me.

Nor would there be a happy ending without my sister Nancy. Determined to spread the word via social media, you did it with precision and force. You had thousands of shares and views on your posts, and that support kept me going. To have you and Laura with me when Oliver jumped into my arms was a moment I will never forget.

My oldest sister, Annette Lubsen, could not participate in our pet-detective work because she lives in Florida. But, Annette, I know if you lived in New York, you would have been in the car with us the day we got Oliver back. We felt the prayers from you and your husband, Bruce, every day.

I received many calls that week from my family who were desperately hoping I would find Oliver. I would like to thank John Johansen, Nancy's husband, and their two children, Jena and Christian, for their support. My sister Annette's children: my niece Colette Reid and her husband, Mike; my niece Brooke Cassens and her husband, Steve; and my nephew Derek Lubsen and his wife, Brook. Thank you for your calls, texts, and notes of support during the most difficult week of my life.

My uncle Pat and aunt Rita, who live in Delaware, thank you for your generosity at a most difficult time in my life. Your support, both monetarily and emotionally, gave my sisters and me a huge boost in our search efforts.

Where would my story be without a literary agent who believed in it? Nena Madonia Oshman of Dupree Miller was that person. We submitted our proposal to her, and she said two words that I will never forget. This story is *precious* and *timeless*. Thank you, Nena and Jan Miller, for believing in me and the story of Oliver.

Where would my story be without a publisher who believed in it as well? Thomas Nelson, a division of HarperCollins Christian Publishing, is that publisher. From day one, they have treated my story with the utmost respect.

A special thank you goes out to Danielle Peterson (associate acquisitions editor), who listened to my story over the phone and believed in its message for young readers from day one.

Thank you, Karissa Taylor (editor), for taking on our story. Your enthusiasm for Oliver has spilled over to your entire team! Everything you have done has made *Oliver* an incredibly special book for young readers. Allowing me the freedom to write Oliver's "thoughts" was one of my favorite projects. Because, as any dog lover knows, dogs have thoughts too!

To Phoebe Wetherbee (interior designer), thank you for creating a beautiful interior to the book. I find it not only engaging for the young reader but for *any* reader who enjoys true creativity.

To Tiffany Forrester (cover art director), what a cover! Oliver practically jumps to life in yellow! Simply fantastic. Sometimes when I'm looking at Oliver in real life, I cannot believe he is *the* dog on that cover. Thank you for such incredible work.

I would like to thank Shaina Fishman (commercial photographer) for taking such beautiful photos of Oliver. The cover of the book is stunning, and you captured his essence perfectly!

A special mention to Lorraine Stundis (photographer); my author photo with Oliver was taken about three months after our being reunited in Mount Vernon. You captured the essence of our happiness together, with Oliver literally smiling! You took so many beautiful photos that day. Thank you.

I would like to give credit to a few people who took photos of Oliver that made it into the book! To Sarah and Leah Dolce, thank you for taking such beautiful portrait photos of Oliver. Also to Jose Cifuentes and Domenic DiSiena from the Shell Gas Station in Bedford, thank you for the photo of Oliver and me next to my Buick and your support when Oliver was missing. And finally, to Eric Weinstein, my friend, thank you for taking the great picture of Oliver and me at your house this past summer.

The credit for the amazing illustration of Oliver goes to Rotem Teplow (illustrator). You captured his essence in your drawing beautifully! Thank you.

A successful book needs a marketing team to make things happen, and once again, Oliver was placed in the hands of true professionals. Thank you to the marketing team: Robin Richardson (senior marketing director) and Natividad Lewis (publicity manager).

To the other professionals who have taken time to proofread and edit my book, thank you for all your hard work: Amy Kerr (copyeditor), Andrew Buss (proofreader), Julie Breihan (proof-reader), and Lisa Grimelstein (proofreader).

There were many key players in holding me together during that fateful week. To Lucy and Alan, thank you for your support. Lucy, for coming to Mount Vernon with us, and Alan, for our talk that most difficult Friday evening and for the pizza delivery on that cold Tuesday night! I have lived in your cottage for nine years, and what incredible lessons I have learned through a simpler life.

Lisa Reyes at News 12, Westchester, thank you for showing up not once but twice! Your interview with me that Friday was simply incredible. We called you, and you showed up with your cameraman in an hour. We called you again when we got Oliver back, and there you were, in Mount Vernon, to celebrate our happiest moment. Thank you and News 12 for the attention you gave my story.

To Eric Weinstein, my friend. We have gone from stuffing newspapers as teenagers to waiting tables as grown men to spending that dismal Saturday together when you came to my rescue to provide me with support. You are a friend indeed. I'll never forget it. I am glad you and Lisa could celebrate Oliver's return with my family!

Tony Marcogliese, you came to our aid on that Tuesday and stayed with us all day and night. Your sudden arrival in Mount Vernon was much needed and appreciated by both me and my sister Laura. Thank you for caring so much about Oliver and me.

Thank you, Isabela Dunlap, for a conversation that turned the tide of our story from bitterness to love. Your compassion and patience with me that evening was exactly what I needed. You spoke from the heart, those words entered my heart, and your comforting words changed my attitude in my search for Oliver.

Janice Connolly, thank you for taking the picture of Oliver that led us to Mount Vernon. Your small act of kindness ignited this story. It should never be forgotten how one small act of kindness can indeed change the world. You did just that.

Manny and Walaa, thank you for taking care of my Oliver. Manny, you rescued him from the street, and Walaa, even though you had two young children to attend to, you took in Oliver and cared for him like he was one of your own. God bless both of you for bringing this story to fruition. You saved my life with your kindness.

Rolando and Terry, the mechanics who helped keep me sane while I climbed fences, walked on rooftops, and searched high and low for Oliver. Thank you for caring about us and showing us the window of support that Mount Vernon gave all of us.

To Mr. Adams, my fourth grade teacher, who made a difference by simply caring enough to get me Harry S. Truman's address. His letter hangs on my wall today as a reminder of who I once thought I could be. Thank you, Mr. Adams, for caring. You created one of the most cherished moments I ever had with my mother. To all the teachers of young people, remember that your extra effort with a student can change their lives forever!

A special thank you to the citizens of Mount Vernon, New York. You let us scour your streets, searching frantically for my Oliver, and offered nothing but kindness. There was no judgment or questioning of our motives. Thank you for treating us with respect and dignity at all times. Maybe that is why Mount Vernon is called the "City of Hope."

To my friends in Bedford whose thoughts and prayers were with me when Oliver was missing—Leif Waller, Michael Winston, Judy Elstein, and Rocco and Nunzio Tripodi.

To my friends at the Bedford Free Library, thank you. You let me wander in there when I first moved to Bedford and quietly mill about the library wondering how to jump-start my life again. Ann, Silvia, and Robyn were most patient with me. You gave me a genuine feeling of community, which I had not felt for a very long time. I want the young readers to always support their local library. Our public libraries are the cornerstones of community.

I cannot thank all my favorite musical artists, because I would need another chapter for that alone. In my worst of moments, I could always depend on music to save me. I have two artists I must mention: Elvis Presley and Sam Cooke. Thank you for dedicating your lives to your craft. Your God-given talents have been loved and cherished by millions.

I would like to acknowledge my best friends in the world, my dogs: Marcie, Coffee, Mickey, Louie, and Oliver. It was your unconditional love that got me here. What a great gift you dogs are to us humans. You have enriched my life, taught me how to cherish the moment, and most importantly, taught me wisdom.

My Oliver, you are loved beyond words can describe. When I look at you, I am amazed—amazed you are with me today, amazed that you love me, and amazed at what I learn from you every day. Thank you, Oliver, for never giving up on me, because I never gave up on you.

Finally, to you, the young reader, thank you for letting me share the story of my life and my love of Oliver. I hope this story resonates in your heart as it did mine. If I have one final word of advice to you, it is this: my imagination saved my life in my darkest moments. Each one of you possesses the incredible ability to use your imagination. Never forget that. It was my imagination that brought Oliver home and gave me this story.

Photography Credits

COVER

FRONT COVER AND SPINE

Oliver headshot: © 2021 Shaina Fishman

BACK COVER

Oliver with his tongue out: © 2021 Sarah and Leah Dolce

Steven and Oliver by a 1951 Buick: © 2021 Jose Cifuentes

Oliver in a tuxedo: ©2021 Steven Carino

PHOTO INSERT

PAGE 1

Top left: Steven's baby photo: Courtesy of Steven Carino

Top right: Steven with his mother: Courtesy of Steven Carino

Middle left: Oliver in a purple scarf: © 2021 Steven Carino

Middle right: Letter from the president: Courtesy of Steven Carino

Bottom left: Steven in a hat: © 2021 Eric Weinstein

Bottom right: Oliver with his tongue out: © 2021 Sarah and Leah Dolce

Page 2

Top left: Oliver in a dog bed: © 2021 Janice Connolly

Top right: Oliver with his tongue out: © 2021 Sarah and Leah Dolce

Middle left: Oliver in the driver's seat: © 2021 Steven Carino

Middle right: Steven and Oliver by a 1951 Buick: © 2021 Jose Cifuentes

Bottom left: Steven and Oliver reunited: © 2021 Walaa Ismail

Page 3

Top left: Oliver with Mickey in the grass: © 2021 Steven Carino

Top right: Oliver in front of a fence: © 2021 Steven Carino

Middle left: Oliver with Mickey at the beach: © 2021 Steven Carino

Middle right: Mickey, Gus, and Oliver: © 2021 Steven Carino

Bottom left: Steven and Oliver on the farm: © 2021 Steven Carino

Bottom right: Oliver in a tuxedo: © 2021 Steven Carino

Page 4

Top left: Oliver in a cart: © 2021 Steven Carino

Top right: Isabela, Oliver, and Steven: © 2021 Steven Carino

Middle left: Oliver eating a dog biscuit: © 2021 Steven Carino

Middle right: Oliver on the couch: © 2021 Steven Carino

Bottom left: Oliver with dinosaur toys: © 2021 Steven Carino

About the Authors

Steven Carino was born in Huntington, New York. The youngest of five children, he graduated from SUNY Brockport with a bachelor of science in American history. He worked as a DJ in New York City before launching careers in advertising and real estate and starting his own employment agency. Today, Steven has his own driving business and lives in a cottage in Bedford, New York, with his best friend, Oliver, and an array of sheep, goats, chickens, a horse, a rooster, and a mini-cow named Anna Belle. *Oliver* is Steven's first book.

Alex Tresniowski is a former human-interest writer at *People* and the bestselling author of several books, most notably *The Vendetta*, which was purchased by Universal Studios and used as a basis for the movie *Public Enemies*. His other titles include *An Invisible Thread*, *Waking Up in Heaven*, and *The Light Between Us*.

Want more Oliver?

There is more to this remarkable story for you and your parent to enjoy!

Get the full story of Oliver's amazing journey

Also available in paperback

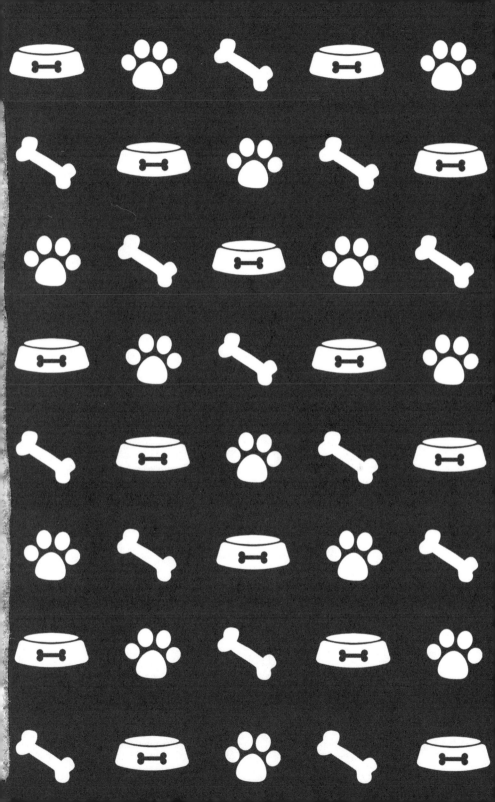